CW01429843

Before Safe Haven: Jules

Christopher Artinian

CHRISTOPHER ARTINIAN

ISBN: 9781655050527

DEDICATION

To the unsung heroes who are forever in our midst.

CHRISTOPHER ARTINIAN

ACKNOWLEDGEMENTS

A very, very big thank you to my better half, Tina. She never, ever lets me down and is always there when I need her.

Massive thanks to the gang across in the fan club on Facebook. I will never get used to the incredible support and loyalty you guys give me. Thank you for everything you do, you're amazing.

Thanks to my editor, Ken, and a massive thank you to the amazing Christian Bentulan, for always designing such amazing covers to accompany these books.

And finally, thank you to you for downloading this book.

1

The days since news that the outbreak had left the quarantine areas and hit the rest of the country had been long, hard and terrifying. No one had really known what to do, especially Jules. She was winging it, but so far, she'd had the Midas touch and people followed her every suggestion. She knew, however, that when they figured out just how clueless she was, the trouble would start.

She watched as her three younger brothers left the manager's office of the Home and Garden Depot. Andy, the eldest, was last to leave and he tripped over the turned-up corner of a carpet tile, grabbing hold of the door frame just in time to avoid falling face down on the floor. Jules shook her head despairingly then looked towards George and Maggie, the two people she had come to rely on more than anyone in the last few days. "I swear to Jesus," she said in her soft Belfast accent, "if I didn't know any better, I'd say my parents were doing crack cocaine when they conceived the three of them. How the fuck can they have come from the same ma and da as me?"

Maggie and George looked at each other and laughed. "Are you sure you weren't adopted?" Maggie asked.

"I tell ya, don't think that thought doesn't keep me up at nights, cos it does. But Ma and Da were good people. If I'd been adopted, they'd have told me. They wouldn't have let me carry on suffering like this." She spun around in her chair to look at her two friends. "Okay, finally to business. How did it go this morning?"

"It was a little tricky," began George, pulling his tobacco pipe from his inside coat pocket and placing it in his mouth.

"Nice try. You're not smoking that in here," Maggie said.

George let out a sigh, took the pipe from his lips and returned it from where it came. Jules smiled. "So anyway, you were saying."

"Yes, we managed to get close to a hundred and twenty gallons from the hot water tanks in surrounding shops and offices. Problem was, though, we got broke off quite a bit. The lookouts did their jobs well though. All in all, it went to plan, but there are a lot more infected around here than there were a couple of days ago," George said.

"Yeah, well, that fire over at the KFC will have brought a lot of attention to the area," Jules said and then turned to Maggie. "How's our pantry looking, Mags?"

"It was looking better before we took in the five newcomers we found in next door's car park yesterday."

It was Jules who sighed this time. "We don't have a choice. We can't leave people out there. And surely the more of us there are, the better chance we have."

"I don't want to sound heartless, and this does sound heartless, but four of those people are in their seventies and only survived this long because up until yesterday morning, they had a working minibus. If it hadn't have been for that young woman with them, none of them would have made it. Having four extra mouths to feed and getting nothing in return doesn't make us stronger, it makes us weaker."

Jules stared at her for a moment. "So, what do you

want me to do, Mags? Turn them away? What kind of person would that make me? What kind of people does it make us?"

"As I said, I know it sounds heartless, but the needs of the many… And I'm just echoing what a lot of people have been saying since they showed up."

"And what do you think?" Jules asked, swivelling in her chair towards George.

"Well, I'm not a million miles away from their age, so I'm probably a bit biased."

"You're different," Maggie said. "You're fit; you contribute as much as anyone … more than anyone."

"Okay, you're biased," Jules said. "I still want to know what you think."

"Well, these people … they were born in the forties. Life would have been hard. Britain had a lot of rebuilding to do after the war. They'll have worked harder than most to make life the best it could be for future generations. I say they've contributed to all of us enough and if they need a hand now, then they should get one. What's more, they'll have knowledge that could be invaluable to us."

"Knowledge about what?" Maggie asked.

"Knowledge about how to live when times were hard, when there were shortages. Simple things but things that would be useful to us now. How not to waste things. People today … everything is throwaway. Back then, nothing was disposable, it was all precious. We need that kind of thinking now, that kind of knowledge."

Maggie shrugged her shoulders, and Jules smiled. "Thank you, George. Those are excellent points."

"Well, don't say I didn't warn you," Maggie said.

"Warn me? Look, if anybody wants to take over, they're more than welcome to. I never wanted to be the leader here. In fact, I'm pretty certain I said it was a fuckin' terrible idea."

"You were a natural choice," George said.

"Why, because I was the deputy manager? Sure, if

we were opening the doors for business, I'd agree; in the absence of the general manager, I'm the perfect person to run things. But just cos I've got a fuckin' set of keys to the place, it doesn't mean I should be making the life and death decisions for all of us."

"I disagree."

"Disagree as much as you want, old man, I'm fuckin' tellin' you."

"You swear a lot, don't you?"

"Fuck you," Jules replied, and they all let out a small laugh.

"Right, I'm heading back down, I'll see you a little later," Maggie said, leaving Jules and George alone.

George watched as the door closed behind her and then turned back to Jules. "The reason people follow you isn't that you're the one with the keys to this place. It's because you're practical yet compassionate at the same time. You're doing a great job, most people think so."

"That's nice of you to say, George, but we'll see if people still feel that way when the food runs out."

"I've been thinking about that."

"And?"

"Well. We've got a couple of conscripts among us, and they were telling me about a quartermaster's store that they visited a few times just a little to the east."

"And?"

George brought his pipe out again. "May I?"

"Doesn't bother me if you want to rot your lungs and smell like my grandad." He smiled and removed a small tin as well. He placed the pipe in his mouth and opened the lid of the tin; pinching a tuft of tobacco between his thumb and forefinger, he tapped it in the chamber and finally lit it. "Jesus Christ, it's like waiting for Christmas."

George took a few puffs making the tobacco crackle and a cloud of blue smoke rise into the air. He put the lid back on the tin, placed the tin in his pocket and pulled the pipe from his mouth, releasing another plume of smoke as he did. "Didn't anyone ever tell you that patience is a virtue, Jules?"

"Didn't anyone ever tell you to get to the bleeding point?"

George smiled, pulled up the chair on the opposite side of the desk and sat down. "Now, where was I?"

"For the love of—"

"Ah yes. Quartermaster's store."

"I swear to God almighty, I'm going to be old and grey before you get to the end of this story."

George ignored her and carried on. "Most people came here with the clothes on their backs and nothing else. There are plenty of places we could get new ones from further in town, but, as we know, that's overrun. Providing it hasn't been raided, we could probably kit out everybody here with a good supply and then some."

"Okay. Can I just ask? Cos I might have missed the point. What the fuck does that have to do with our food supply?"

"I was coming to that."

"When?"

"Directly."

"Jaysus."

"Also, at the quartermaster's, there are weapons and ammunition. Now, as our food supplies dwindle, we're going to have to become increasingly bold with our ventures to find more, so I think having a small band of trained guards will be integral not just to our scavenging trips but also to the security of this place." He put the pipe back in his mouth and took another long suck before releasing another billowing cloud of blue smoke.

"See, that's why you should be running this place and not me. You think of all the important shite I could never even fathom."

"I'm a doer, I'm not a leader."

"Yeah, but people listen to you, George. You have the respect of everybody in this building."

"As do you."

"But you know what you're doing."

George smiled. "I have faith in you, Jules; have a little faith in yourself."

Suddenly, the door burst open, and Maggie rushed in. "Jesus Christ," Jules said, putting her hand up to her chest, "are you trying to give us a bleedin' heart attack?"

"We've got a problem," said Maggie.

"Yeah, tell me about it, I think I just pissed myself."

"I'm serious."

"What is it?" George said, turning slowly in his seat to look at Maggie.

"Stephen, Jeff and Clive are all gone. They've taken their families with them."

"That's not such a big problem. All they did was complain about everything anyway and shirk whatever work they could," Jules said.

"That's not what I'm concerned about."

"What is it then?"

"Jules, they've taken most of the supplies. We won't have enough to see us to the end of the week."

2

Jules and George looked at each other as the full weight of Maggie's words sunk in. The smoke continued to drift in the room, making the atmosphere even heavier.

"How the fuck did that happen?" Jules asked, standing up from the desk, sending her chair wheeling across the carpet.

"Looks like everybody else was busy, washing clothes, preparing dinner, the usual stuff. I went to the storeroom, after our discussion I decided it might be an idea to take an inventory, but—"

"So what? They just walked out with it under their arms?" Jules asked.

"This is my fault," George said.

"Your fault?" Jules asked. "How is this your fault?"

"Clive was a mechanic. He mentioned something yesterday about being able to get the minibus that the newcomers were in moving again. I thought it was about time he did something useful and told him to go ahead by all means. I didn't realise it was part of some plan to run off with our supplies."

"Brilliant. So we've got until the end of the week to get fresh supplies, or we all start going hungry," Jules said.

Maggie pulled up a chair as well, and they all just sat around the desk staring into space. Eventually, George stood up, taking another long puff on his pipe. He walked across to the window and stared out contemplatively. "Seems to me that we're going to have to head to that quartermaster's sooner rather than later."

"Quartermaster's?" Maggie asked. "So, you've discussed it then?"

"Thought it seemed prudent."

Maggie turned to Jules. "What do you think about the idea?"

"What I think becomes less and less relevant by the minute. We're up Shit Creek without a paddle in a boat with holes in it."

"You do have a wonderful way with words," George said.

"It's a gift."

"Seemingly."

Jules looked at her watch then looked towards Maggie. "Who else knows this? About the food. I mean."

"Lizzy was with me when I was doing the stocktake, but I told her not to say a word to anyone until I spoke to you."

"Lizzy? Oh shite. She's nothing but a gob on a stick. The whole fuckin' store'll know by now. George, it's three o'clock. How many people do you think we need to go to the quartermaster's place? And how soon do you think they can be ready?"

"You want to go today?"

"Yeah, I want to go today. If people think we're running low on food, who's to say more won't get the idea of running out?"

George had one final puff on his pipe and levered open the window. He turned the chamber upside down and tapped it on the ledge, watching the spent tobacco and a few sparks drift onto the canopy of the loading bay below. "I dare say we can have a group ready in twenty minutes or so."

"Well, dare say and make it happen, me and Mags will meet you down there."

George nodded and left, leaving the two women together. "Are you okay?" Maggie asked.

"What possible reason would there be for me not to be okay?"

Maggie smiled. "Okay, stupid question," she said, getting up. "I'll see you down there."

Jules swivelled in her chair and looked out of the open window into the blue sky. She had never wanted this kind of responsibility. She fell into the deputy manager role by accident, and now she was sitting in the manager's chair with much more at stake than a healthy balance sheet. The door opened again, but Jules didn't turn around.

Footsteps came up behind her, and a gentle hand moved onto her shoulder, around her neck and down the front of her T-shirt. "Men these days have no fuckin' finesse, do they? Just straight in there, not as much as a hello."

"I'm sorry," the man said, beginning to remove his hand.

Jules slapped her own hand over his, pinning it against her skin. "I didn't say stop now, did I?"

The two of them giggled. The man withdrew his hand, and Jules spun around in her chair. "Hi!"

"Hi, gorgeous," Jules replied, standing up and throwing her arms around him. The two of them shared a long, passionate kiss before Jules pulled back and stared dreamily at him. Benicio was Spanish by birth. His handsome Latin features were accentuated by a smile that no matter how dire a situation was managed to light up a room.

He moved his hand up to Jules's face and gently flicked away a curl of red hair from her forehead before kissing it. "Hello, beautiful," he said, smiling and revealing teeth whiter than snow.

"Boy, are you a sight for sore eyes?"

"Bad day?"

"Bad century. I think I'd have been much happier if I'd have been born a couple of hundred years ago. All this women's lib shite I can do without. What's wrong with men running around after me, treating me like a fuckin' princess and me just sipping tea and planning dinner parties?"

Benicio smiled. "Life is so unfair."

"It totally fuckin' is," Jules said, smiling, and they both kissed again.

Their lips finally parted, and Benicio pulled Jules towards him. "So we're heading out?"

"Yeah," Jules replied, pressing her ear to his chest and listening to his heart beat.

"I don't suppose there's any point in me trying to convince you to stay here?"

"What and miss out on all the fun?"

"You take too many risks, Jules."

"Ben, darlin', you're a sweetheart, but people look to me. If I come up with plans and let other people carry them out while I stay here, safe, what kind of message does that send?"

"You have done enough. You don't need to prove anything. Everybody knows you are a good person; you are brave, you are fair."

"Aww, stop it, you're making my head big."

"I am being serious."

"I know you are, but I couldn't do it in good conscience. I couldn't let people take risks on my behalf. It wouldn't be right."

He moved both his hands up to her cheeks and just looked at her for a moment. "I have never met a girl like you."

"Hey, you've only known me a week. I'm saving up all the good stuff," she replied with a cheeky grin.

"Do you think we can sneak up here again tonight, just you and me, when everybody else is asleep?"

"I think we might manage that." They kissed again. "Now, come on, we've got work to do."

George and Maggie walked straight up to Jules and Ben as they both appeared through the *staff only* door. "We've got thirteen volunteers including you two, Maggie and myself. We can take—"

"I want you to stay here, Mags," Jules interrupted, turning towards the older woman.

"Why?"

"I need somebody smart, who people will listen to, to take care of things and avert any disasters."

"On the subject of which, your brothers all volunteered," Maggie replied.

"In which case, it's more important than ever that you stay here. The chances of us not returning just went up threefold."

"Come on, they're not that bad."

"We'll see soon enough, won't we?"

"It'll be fine," Maggie replied.

*

Jules and Ben sat in the passenger seats of the first box van, scouring the landscape as George accelerated out of the city. Several creatures ran towards them and battered themselves against the vehicle, but the van was travelling at enough speed for them not to be a threat. The convoy was heading east out of the city, and they knew the majority of the infected were concentrated in the centre. They knew this not because they had seen them, but every time they stepped outside there was a constant, chilling, growling dirge that made the air vibrate as if legions of Lucifer's demons were just waiting for the right moment to unleash hell on earth. Stragglers here and there gravitated towards it, and it was a handful of those stragglers that rushed towards the box vans now. Thud! Thud! Thud! Thud! The spinning bodies flew off the sides of the vehicles, landing in crumpled heaps on kerbs and verges.

It took George less than four minutes to clear the

city outskirts. The tension in the cab eased as an industrial landscape gave way to fields and hedgerows. The afternoon sun continued to shine and, provided they did not look in the wing mirrors towards the city behind them and the fading smoke plumes, they could forget they were in the middle of the apocalypse.

"How far is this place?" Jules asked.

"Not too far," George replied.

"Oh, right, thanks for clearing that up."

"It's a few miles. I know the place. I was just never bored enough to measure the distance from the town centre."

"I wonder how Olly's getting on back there with my brothers."

"Well, considering he's the only one who owns a rifle and we haven't heard any shots yet, I can only assume that's a good sign."

"Fair point," Jules replied.

The journey continued in silence until they reached a tall chain-link fence. George slowed the box van down to a stop, and they all looked towards the even taller grassy bank behind it, hiding whatever lay beyond. He started the van moving again, slower this time. The chain links were punctuated by weathered signs; *Ministry of Defence Property. No admittance to unauthorised personnel.*

They came to a left turn, and George manoeuvred the vehicle around the corner. The fence-lined road led to an equally tall and sturdy looking gate. Behind it, there was a sentry box and access barrier, but there was no sign of a sentry guard. George pulled on the handbrake, and the three of them climbed out. There was another notice on this gate, a little more threatening in tone.

MINISTRY OF DEFENCE PROPERTY. KEEP OUT.

This is a prohibited place within the meaning of the official secrets act. Unauthorised persons entering this area may be arrested and prosecuted.

"Not the warmest of welcomes," Jules said.

"Seems a bit over the top for a quartermaster's store, doesn't it?" Ben said.

"Yes ... yes it does," George replied.

They heard the rear door of the first box van open and somebody jump down.

"This wasn't on here before," Olly said, walking up to join them.

"How long ago was it since you came?" George asked.

"I dunno, maybe five or six months."

"Looks like they might have been doing something here other than dishing out supplies," Jules said.

"It's a big place. We only ever went to the main reception in building A. There were barracks, underground bunkers and all sorts that we never got to see. I heard that when the army was called back to defend the capital, though, everybody stationed here went down there and the place was abandoned."

"So, you're telling me they might have taken all the supplies down there with them?" Jules asked.

"Well, it's possible, but if you got an emergency order calling you to London, would you think it was a logistical priority to make sure surplus uniforms and bedding were on the trucks?"

"Fair point," George replied. "No harm in us having a little look around anyway."

"Yeah, famous last words," Jules replied. "How come you didn't get the order, Olly?"

"Who says I didn't?" he replied with a smile on his face.

"Come on then, let's get to work," George said.

Jules sighed. "Okay. We're going to need the bolt cutters, though, by the look of it."

Olly walked back to the rear of the van. "Bolt cutters," he said, no please, no thank you. The amiable man who spoke to Jules, George and Ben suddenly disappeared.

Andy, Rob and Jon, Jules's brothers, climbed down from the back of the truck. Rob, the middle brother, carried the bolt cutters and walked towards the chained gate with the others behind him.

"I don't think—"

"Don't worry," Rob said, interrupting George, "I know what I'm doing."

George let out a sigh and reached into his coat pocket for his pipe while the three brothers walked up to the chain. He went through his ritual of carefully loading the chamber and lighting the brown flakes, inhaling deeply until they caught. He withdrew the pipe from his mouth and looked towards Olly with a smile on his face. Olly just shook his head.

"What am I missing?" Jules asked.

"You'll see, poppet," George replied.

They watched as the three brothers approached the thick, heavy-duty chain and padlock, which secured the gate. Rob opened the cutters and clamped the blades around one of the chunky links, squeezing the handles together with every grain of strength he had. The blades did not move. "You're doing it wrong," Andy said.

"Am not," Rob replied.

"Are too. Give them here," Andy said, snatching the bolt cutters from his brother and placing the blades on a different link. He grunted as he fixed the sharp edges around the thick metal and tried to force the handles together.

"See, they're bust, there's something wrong with them."

"Let me try," Jon said.

"Get lost," replied Andy. "If I can't do it, there's no way you'll be able to."

"Will too."

Jules let out a breath. "God, give me the strength to overcome the trials you set me in this life." She turned towards George. "Please make this stop. One way or another. Open the gate, kill them, kill me, just make it stop, I can't take any more."

George took another long puff on his pipe, clamped the plastic bit between his teeth and walked to the cab of the box van. He returned a few seconds later with a much bigger set of bolt cutters and, while the three brothers were still arguing with each other, walked up to the chain. He extended the thirty-six-inch tool and clipped the galvanised steel links as if he was clipping a fingernail. There was a loud metallic clunk as the chain unravelled and fell to the ground, and George walked the gate inwards. He strode over to the yellow-and-black barrier post and examined it for a moment before opening a small door. He removed a handle, positioned it in a slot on the side of the post and began to crank it around. With each turn, the barrier rose a little further until it was vertical. He sucked hard on his tobacco pipe once more, a reward for a job well done, then returned to the box van and climbed in.

Andy, Rob and Jon looked on a little bewildered before returning to the back of the van. "I think I might just walk in from here," Olly said, unslinging his SA80.

"Can't say I blame you, but don't you think we should all stick together?" Jules replied.

Olly looked back towards the van. "Tell you what," Ben said, "you sit up front with George and Jules, I'll get into the back with the three stooges."

"You've just become one of my favourite people," Olly replied. Not waiting to be asked twice, he walked to the passenger side of the cab and got in.

"Thanks, darlin'," Jules said.

"Doesn't seem right Olly having to suffer like that. We should sit with them in shifts," Ben said, smiling.

"Olly having to suffer? What do I get for my lifetime of suffering?"

"Well, I'm sure we can figure something out tonight."

Jules giggled like a schoolgirl. "I'll hold you to that."

She leaned in and kissed him on the cheek. "See you in a couple of minutes."

They boarded the van and the two vehicles set off once again. The fence ended after the gate, but the tall grass banks continued, concealing whatever hid behind them. The road led to an expansive network of carparks and buildings. The tall grass embankment surrounded all of it, making sure it was only visible in its entirety by air.

"Okay, we want to be just over there," Olly said, pointing.

George turned the wheel and brought the van to a stop outside of an austere looking brown brick building. He pulled on the handbrake, looked around slowly and deliberately, and then turned the key in the ignition, silencing the engine. The second box van pulled up behind them, and all the occupants climbed out.

A few seconds later, the twelve men and women were gathered in a circle. "Okay, Olly's been here before; he's the one who'll be guiding us. Remember, we don't know what to expect, so keep your eyes peeled." Jules turned from person to person. She saw the fear in their eyes as they held on to the pick-axe handles, hatchets and garden forks they had brought as weapons. She looked down towards the small axe she held in her own hand and felt the same apprehension, but she could not show it. She was their leader; she had to be strong, confident. She had to give them hope. "Before you know it, we'll be back at the Home and Garden Depot with new clothes, better weapons and a big bowl of Mary Stolt's stew for supper." She got a small ripple of laughter from the assembled crowd; then she turned towards Olly. "Okay, darlin', lead on."

Olly walked up to the aluminium and glass double doors. He raised the butt of his rifle, ready to smash one of the tall panes when something made him stop. He reached out his hand and pulled the long vertical handle. The door shifted outwards, and he shot an urgent glance back to Jules. "Erm, looks like someone forgot to lock up."

"At an M.O.D. base? With big threatening trespass signs everywhere."

"Our luck might be changing," Olly replied.

"Oh yeah, I'm sure that's it." Jules turned to the others. "Nobody goes anywhere by themselves. Make sure you're always paired up at least."

Olly advanced through the entrance with his rifle raised. There was plenty of light in the reception area, but the hallways beyond were shadowy. He ignored the long corridors to the left and right, and the hair on his arms bristled as he proceeded beyond the front desk and left the warm comfort of the sun's beams. He heard the others following and felt a presence at either side of him. Olly turned to see Ben to his left, clutching a pitchfork. To his right was Jules, gripping the handle of a hatchet.

The group proceeded down the main corridor towards a set of double doors. Ben reached out ready to push one open when he suddenly stopped. "What is it?" asked Olly.

"Can you hear something?" Ben replied.

"Something like what?" Jules asked.

"It sounds like ... growling."

3

It was almost as if the words themselves made the corridor turn darker. George shuffled his way to the front to join Jules, Ben and Olly. He flicked on the beam of a powerful torch and shone it through the glass panel in the left door. They looked through the right one to avoid the reflection, and all four of them turned to stone. It was like a scene from a horror movie. Red streaks painted desperate swirls on the walls and pools of dried blood blotted the linoleum tiles.

"Okay," Jules said, "I'm officially calling this mission off. Let's get back to the—"

"Infected!" shouted someone at the back of the group.

They all turned to see four figures emerging from the left corridor next to reception. They were quickly followed by two more appearing from the right.

"Shite!" Jules cried, immediately turning back to the doors and flinging them open. "Everybody move, now."

Olly, Ben and George ran through to the other side, turning back around straight away, readying themselves to fight. Olly raised his rifle, knowing if he pulled the trigger, it would already be too late. If there were six of these things, no doubt there would be more and a single shot would alert every last one of them as to the group's whereabouts. The team filtered through, one by one. Jules snatched the pick-axe handle Andy was carrying ready to feed it through the door handles. It wasn't perfect, but it might block the progress of the creatures long enough for them to find another way out. Just then, she noticed a lone figure standing perfectly still, looking towards the beasts storming towards her like a baby rabbit trapped in the frightening glare of car headlights.

Jules understood the woman's terror; she understood the morbid fascination as these monsters that could surely be from no other place than hell itself tore towards her. She handed the pick-axe handle to George and ran forward, grabbing the woman tightly by the arm and spinning her around. "I—" the woman began to say.

"Run! Now!" Jules commanded.

The woman snapped out of her horror-induced catatonia and sprinted through the doors, with Jules still clenching her upper arm. The charging monsters were no more than five metres behind as they crossed the threshold. Olly and Ben forced the doors shut and George wedged the thick wooden shaft through the handles. There was a deafening bang as three creatures smashed against the double doors in almost choreographed synchronicity. The other three came in a second wave, and the pick-axe handle rattled and shifted as the beasts battered themselves against the solid wood.

Rob had been entrusted with the torch, and now he shone it towards one of the slim glass panels. One of the infected had the side of its face pressed up against it. The eerie pallid hue of its skin chilled the blood of everyone present. Its jet-black pupil flared on the milky grey surface of its eyeball and the woman who had been transfixed by these things seconds before now let out an embarrassed whimper as she lost control of her bladder and the air around the group filled with the sour odour of urine.

"That door's not going to hold forever," George said.

"Jesus, Rob! Point that thing somewhere else for Christ's sake," Jules said.

For a moment, Rob did not move. The words had not even registered. He was as mesmerised as everybody else with the grotesque creature caught in the torch's ray. Finally, he came to his senses, looked towards his sister and turned, moving the beam down the hallway. There were multiple doors, and all of them were closed, meaning the torchlight was the only source of illumination.

"I'm assuming there's a fire exit," George said, trying to be heard over the sound of the monsters still hammering at the door.

The battery backup for the emergency exit signs had long since run dry, but Rob panned the flashlight around and soon managed to find the way out. "This building is shaped like a giant letter H," Olly said. "Right now, we're in the centre of the connecting line. These rooms on either side are storerooms." He turned towards Jules. "I can stay here and guard the door; we can still get what we came for."

"It's too much of a risk. Fresh togs and a few other bits and pieces aren't worth anyone getting killed for. We'll—" There was another cacophonous bang as all of the beasts smashed against the doors at the same time. One of the women and two of the men let out frightened screams. "As I was saying, let's get the fuck out of here." Jules placed her hand on Rob's back and guided him down the hallway. "Come on."

The group started to run, doing their best to ignore the bloody murals on the walls. They were halfway down the hall when a dark figure emerged up ahead of them. "Oh shite," Jules said, placing her arm out to stop her brother's advance and thus bringing the rest of the party to a sudden halt too. Jules clutched the hatchet even harder in her hand and stepped forward. She knew this was their only way out, and she was the leader. She waited for the charge, but Ben, Olly, George and her three brothers all crowded the hallway alongside her. They would not let Jules face this alone.

A few seconds passed, but the silhouette at the end of the hall remained statuesque. "Who are you?" it eventually said, breaking the silence and stepping forward into the light.

Jules loosened the grip on her weapon a little despite the fact the figure, now emerging into the arc of light a little more, was clearly holding a rifle. "We're just looking for a way out of here, away from those ... things."

"Follow me," he said, flicking his own torch on.

Jules, Ben, Olly and George all looked at one another then glanced back towards the shuddering doors. "Come on," Jules said, then whispered, "don't let your guards down."

The group ran along the hall towards the T-junction then followed the figure as he disappeared into one of the rooms. He flicked his torch off, and Rob followed suit as natural light bled in through the high, narrow, frosted glass windows. The door clunked shut behind them. It was a giant pantry. Many of the metal racks and shelves were empty, but at the far end of the room, there were others that were still filled with tins and packets.

"What is this place?" Andy asked.

The figure who had led them from the hallway turned to look at him with a creased brow. "What does it look like?"

"Like a big pantry."

"Well, you're obviously not as stupid as you look."

"I'd hold back judgement on that if I were you," Jules said.

The burly figure cracked a thin smile beneath his black beard. "Who is it, Rog?" came another voice from behind one of the shelving units.

"Just figuring that one out, Scotty."

"Listen," Jules said, looking at the uniform Rog was

wearing, "we're just trying to find a way out of this place."

"I'm interested why you're here in the first place."

"That's down to me," Olly replied. "I came here once."

"You in the service?" Scotty asked.

"Briefly. Didn't get much of a crack at it before everything turned to shit."

"Me and Scotty have got twenty years between us."

"Are you the only ones here?"

Another loud bang echoed down the hallway from the double doors. "Well, not the only ones," Scotty replied, nodding his head in the direction of the sound.

"What happened?" Jules asked.

"You probably heard about the last stand to save the capital. Everything happened so quickly, it was such a mess. Well, a group of us were ordered to stay behind for twenty-four hours, to make sure all the remaining food, every last gun, every last bullet got loaded and sent south. I'm sure you can imagine, as soon as the top brass left, all hell broke loose. Five men got in a truck that first night and made a run for it. Needless to say, that started others thinking about doing the same. Problem was, though, those men didn't get very far. Three of them ended up back here on foot. Didn't realise at the time, though, that one of them had been bitten on the arm. The bastard kept it well hidden. Well, you can guess what happened next. Another group tried to make a run for it, and Scotty did his best to stop them. They ran straight over him, two broken legs just like that. We've been here ever since."

"Just the two of you?" Jules asked.

"Yeah," Rog said, leading the group around the racking to see a figure lying on the floor with a half-bottle of whisky and a packet of painkillers by his side. His legs had been strapped to two makeshift splints, and his face was badly bruised.

"Hi," Scotty said.

"Shite, you look like you've been through a

mangle," Jules said.

"Funny, that's exactly how I feel too."

"So, you're the only two who stayed?" Jules said.

"Didn't really have a choice. Scotty couldn't go anywhere, and I wasn't going to leave my best mate."

Jules gave Rog a long, respectful look, but it was George who spoke next. "There's something I don't understand. The gates were chained and padlocked when we arrived here. It seems strange that your friends—"

"No fucking friends of mine," interrupted Rog.

"Your colleagues, then, would take the time to stop and padlock the gates shut."

"That was me. First and last time I went out there."

"How did you get out?" Jules asked.

Rog nodded towards the windows. "Climbed the racking and lowered myself down. There's a recycling bin just on the other side."

"Why? If you don't mind me asking," George asked.

"I figured we didn't want to be facing any more of those things. What if a horde of them came through the gate?"

"Err—" George began with a slightly confused look on his face.

"I realised pretty quickly that those things were already spread out all over the grounds, but we didn't want to be entertaining any more. The day we shut ourselves in here, I saw some in the building; until I heard your commotion today, I didn't head back in there either," he said, nodding towards the door.

"How many do you think there are in total?" Jules asked.

"Twenty-five or so."

"Twenty-five?" Jules asked, shocked.

"At a guess."

"And what's your plan?"

"Haven't really got one. I mean this is as good a

place as any to live out the last days on Earth, isn't it?"

"These are hardly the last days on Earth," Jules replied.

"You could have fooled me."

"We were so close as well," said Scotty. "We had a half-loaded truck out there. Food, weapons, supplies. We just needed to load up the rest of it, and then we'd have been on our way. Just a few more hours."

"A truck?" Jules said.

"Yeah," replied Scotty, picking up the whisky and taking a drink.

"Look," she said, turning towards Rog, "we came here looking for clothes and supplies. By the sound of it, that truck more than takes care of the supplies part. Help us, and we can all get out of here together."

Rog looked down at Scotty, who was wiping his mouth and placing the top back on the bottle. "Can I speak to you?" he said to Jules in a hushed tone.

The pair of them walked off to one side, while the others began to look around at the array of food on the shelves.

"What is it?" Jules asked when they were out of hearing distance.

"The truck's no good."

"What do you mean the truck's no good?"

"It won't work, it's trashed."

"I don't understand. Who would trash it?"

Rog let out a long sigh and bowed his head. He looked back in the direction of the others then towards Jules. "Me."

"I really don't have a clue what you're talking about. Why would you trash your only means of—" Jules broke off and glanced towards Scotty, who had half a smile on his face as the effects of the whisky began to kick in. "You didn't chain the gate to stop any of those things getting in. You chained it to prevent yourself from leaving. And you trashed the truck because it was too much of a temptation."

Rog looked ashamed. "I'd given Scotty plenty of painkillers, anti-inflammatories and he'd had about a quarter of a bottle of single malt too. He was out for the count. I got into that truck, and I started driving. I reached the gate and…"

"Most people would have carried on."

"I was so close. Anyway, I grabbed the chains and padlock from the gatehouse, chained it all up and literally threw away the key. I drove back here, had a few of those things following me by that time too. I knew if I left the truck in working order, it would be too much of a temptation for me; when things got desperate, I'd try driving through the gate. So, I shredded the tyres and ripped out the wiring. There's no way that rig is going anywhere."

"You're a decent man, Rog."

"No, no, I'm not. A decent man would never have even thought about leaving a friend in the first place."

"We all have weak moments."

"Don't make excuses for me."

Jules looked at him long and hard. "It doesn't have to end like this for either of you. We're getting out of here, and you can come with us. There are two box vans waiting at the front of this building. If we can get past those six things out there waiting for us, then we stand a chance."

"There's no way Scotty can make it, and I'm not leaving without him."

Jules thought for a moment. "What about if we rigged him some kind of stretcher?"

Suddenly, the impossible seemed a little more possible. "We've holed up at the Home and Garden Depot in Inverness. There are a good number of us. We've got our problems, but it's better than this. It's better than just waiting to die."

Rog thought for a moment. "Okay. Okay, we'll do it."

Jules smiled and placed a reassuring hand on his arm. She walked over to the others. "Rog and Scotty are going to be coming back home with us."

"What about those things out there?" Jon asked.

"We're going to figure that out," Jules replied.

"Jules, it seems stupid leaving all this behind," Olly said, gesturing around at all the food.

"I don't know if you've noticed, darlin', but we're not in the strongest of positions at the moment. There are six of those things in the building and God knows how many more out there. The sooner we get out of here, the sooner we'll be safe."

"I understand what you're saying, but listen to me a minute. If we leave all this, we'll only have to find food from somewhere else and who's to say that won't be more dangerous? Every time we come out, it's a risk, we know that. Right now, though, we're in a place that can solve our food problems, our clothing problems and our weapons problems. I say we clear this place then help ourselves."

Jules looked towards Ben then at George. "What do you say?"

George rubbed his fingers over his whiskered face. "I think Olly makes a good point."

"Twenty-five you say?" Jules asked, looking towards Rog.

"There or thereabouts."

She looked around at the rest of the faces who were all staring back at her. "Let's do this."

4

The plan took form quickly. There wasn't a soul who did not want to be back at the Home and Garden Depot before nightfall. The six creatures continued to batter against the double doors, and as the group headed back out with their pitchforks and various makeshift weapons, they saw that the sturdy piece of wood that had been slid through the door handles had nearly been rattled free.

Olly and Rog positioned themselves at either side of the group with their weapons raised; they had no intention of firing unless it was an absolute last resort. They were the only two who had been trained to use the rifles, and although Scotty's SA80 was leaning against the wall in the pantry, it was more of a liability than an asset in the hands of someone who did not know how to use it.

Rob shone the torch towards the doors, and the group just stood there looking for a moment. Jules gulped and walked up to the doors. Her hand shook as she jiggled the thick wooden pick-axe handle back to the centre to ensure the doors did not burst open and allow the beasts through while they carried out the first part of their plan. She looked back to the rest of the group. They were all just silhouettes in the perimeter of the torchlight, but these silhouettes were the only real hope the other occupants of the Home and Garden Depot had.

Jules turned back to the doors. She raised her hatchet and smashed it against the narrow glass panel on the right, immediately shattering the pane and filling the hallway with the hellish growling chorus. Almost immediately, one of the creatures extended its arm, its fingers grabbing, desperate to touch the sweet-smelling pink flesh of the young woman in front of it.

Jules instinctively jumped back as the hand extended into the darkness towards her. Even in the shadowy light cast by the torch, she could see the unnatural greyness of the creature's skin and a shiver ran down her spine. Its fingers continued to snap at the air like a shark's jaws frantically trying to wrap themselves around their prey. Then Jules saw a shadow from behind her looming closer. Ben appeared at her side before raising his pitchfork and thrusting it through the head of the beast. The full beam of the torch shone towards the creature as he withdrew the fork once more.

If it had been a human he had stabbed, fountains of blood would have issued forth from the wounds, but these things were different. The blood was almost congealed, and the prongs came out with a sickening slurping sound. The creature fell back only to be replaced by another, anxious to take its turn at claiming a prize.

This time Jules darted forward, parrying the reaching arm and making her hatchet blade whistle as it sliced through the air towards its target. There was a crack, which reverberated through the entire hallway as the small axe shattered the skull of its victim. Jules tugged hard, pulling the weapon back out just as quickly before skipping backwards once more as a third monster appeared in the narrow aperture.

Andy ran forward, desperate to prove his worth. He grabbed hold of the monster's stretching arm, removing the threat of it clutching him as he dealt with it. He brought the clawhammer down hard on its head. The first blow only stunned it, but then he brought it down again, harder. Another stomach-turning crack echoed up and down the corridor as the face and neck of the hammer disappeared into the creature's head. He whipped it back out and a small piece of brain and bone fragment danced in the torch beam for a moment before finally falling to the ground. The beast slumped a little, its thick shoulder wedged in the narrow gap. Andy tentatively pushed at it to clear the way, but the dead creature did not move.

Just then, another grasping hand shot through the opening clutching Andy by the upper arm. He let out a scream, immediately drowning out the growls and the banging of the rest of the beasts. Olly took aim, ready to fire, but Jules and Ben both shot to Andy's aid.

Ben grabbed him, pulling him backwards while Jules hacked the creature's arm, unable to reach its head because of the other beast, which was still blocking much of the opening. The small axe blade burrowed into the elbow joint, once, twice, third time was the charm, as Andy and Ben both fell backwards. The beast's arm now hung from the elbow down like a dangling piece of soaked cloth; completely useless, nothing more than a gory ornament. It withdrew its flopping limb and turned to use its other arm.

It was George who came forward now with his heavy shovel. He got down low and thrust it into the gap, knocking the wedged creature out of place and the reaching beast off balance.

Ben and Andy climbed back to their feet, and the four of them made short work of the remaining attackers. The creatures fell, and enough natural light seeped through for Rob to be able to turn the torch off. Jules, Ben, Andy and George spent a few seconds trying to catch their breath before removing the pick-axe handle, pulling open the doors and continuing down the corridor.

Jules placed a gentle hand on Andy's back as they walked. "That was a really brave thing you did."

"You're my sister. I'll never let you face a fight alone."

Jules's face warmed. "I love you, y'know?"

"Yeah, well ... same here."

"Don't get me wrong. Most of the time, you do nothing but get on my tits," she said, smiling, "but I love you, Rob and Jon like you wouldn't believe. You're my family and nothing's more important than that."

They emerged into the foyer and, Andy looked across at her. "I know." They both smiled and then the tenderness was over. Jules was back to being the group leader.

She looked towards Ben. "Are you sure you want to do this?"

"Want to?" he said, smiling. "This isn't even in the top ten thousand things I want to do, but it's the best plan."

Rog walked up behind them. "Remember what I said, carry straight on, turn right and then you've got six big dormitories that you can just weave around. Keep leaving gaps in between hitting the horn and listen out for our signal. When we're loaded, you come back here; then I'll take over. We'll get your van loaded up too and then we can get the hell out of here."

Ben nodded. "I've got my bodyguard anyway," he said, nodding towards Olly.

"Don't worry, Jules, I'll keep him in one piece for you. Of course, we all know what piece that is," Olly said with a cheeky grin and the others laughed.

"Well, you just make sure you do," she said, smiling. "Both of you be careful, and we'll see you soon."

The two men walked up to the first box van. Ben climbed into the driver's seat, Olly got into the passenger side, and the engine started. They manoeuvred in a slow circle, and the loud horn began to sound. The rest of the group stayed well back from the doors, ready to make an escape down the hall if something went wrong, and rather than following the box van, the creatures sped towards the entrance of the building.

Slowly the beasts emerged, one by one then two by two until eventually there were over twenty charging towards the van. The tension in the entrance hall was palpable, and the speed and ferocity of the undead horde made more than one or two of them gasp. Jules felt a gentle hand wrap around her wrist. "Don't worry, sunshine, they'll be fine," George said.

She looked across towards him and placed her other hand over his. They all continued to watch until the van, and the beasts were out of sight; then George and Rog headed out to the second van. "Right, you lot," Jules said, "we need to get this done as quickly as possible. Food and water first, clothes and the rest of the supplies after."

They marched back down the corridor as the sound of the horn became fainter. Rob took the lead, guiding them with the torch. They reached the pantry and Scotty called out, clearly a little squiffy due to the combination of painkillers and alcohol. "That you, Roger Dodger?"

"It's Jules." She walked around the racking and stood over him. "Are there any trolleys or carts that we can use to transport this stuff?" she asked, gesturing towards the shelving units.

"Absotively posolutely," he said, letting out a small chuckle. "Next door, in the mess and the kitchen, you'll find all sorts. That fire door will be the best one to use to get all the gear out too. Now don't you forget about me, will you?" he said, pointing his finger but failing to keep it still.

"Don't worry, darlin', we're not going anywhere without you."

"I like you, Jules, you've got a kind face."

"That's sweet of you to say. I like you too and don't you worry, we're going to have you back at the Depot in no time, and we'll see if we can make things a little more comfortable for you."

"How? Have you got more scotch there?"

Jules smiled. "Not what I was thinking, but we'll

see what we can do." She turned around to look at the others. "Okay, you heard the man, the trolleys are next door, let's get moving." She started to walk out then stopped. "Wouldn't it have made sense to have a door running through from here to the kitchen?"

Scotty took another sip of whisky. "Things got out of hand here. This place used to be a training room, but when we started getting recruits from all over the country, we soon realised we needed a bigger pantry. A door was on the list of things to do, but time caught up with us." Now Scotty seemed a little less tipsy and more introspective. "I suppose time caught up with everybody."

Jules turned to see that the others had all left the room in search of the trolleys. "Yeah, I suppose it did." She started to head out too.

"It would have been my Louise's eighteenth this month," he said, quietly.

Jules stopped. "Is she…?"

"Dead? The wife and I parted company a long time ago. She took the kids, not really practical for me to, doing what I do." He looked up towards Jules. "I was going to take leave. The ex and me used to get on well enough. We went in halves for a big surprise birthday bash for her."

"Do you know for a fact they didn't make it?"

Scotty unscrewed the top of the bottle again and took another drink. "They lived in Portsmouth."

His words hung in the air like the smell of rotting meat. Portsmouth was the first city to be quarantined in the UK and Ireland. The world had gone to hell and for months Great Britain had staved off infection. Jules remembered back to the day … the second when she had heard the broadcast on the news. She bent down and took the bottle from Scotty's hand. "To your daughter and your family. May their souls be at peace. Sláinte," Jules said before taking a drink. She handed the bottle back to Scotty.

He raised the bottle in front of him just as Jules had. "Sláinte."

By the time they had finished their toasts, the first of the trolleys were being wheeled in from the kitchen. "Back at the Depot, we have a little remembrance plot," she said as she watched eager hands grabbing plastic-wrapped trays of tins from the shelves and loading them onto the carts.

"What do you mean?" Scotty asked.

"The garden section of the Depot is behind a massive walled area with fences climbing another dozen feet higher than that, so there's no danger of the infected ever seeing us or bothering us. We've got rows of plant pots in there with people's names written on. If we had a church, we'd light candles for our dead, but I thought it might be nice if people were able to sow a seed for their loved ones. A way to remember them. You probably think it's daft, but a lot of us have done it."

"I don't think it's daft at all," Scotty replied. "I'd very much like to do that for my family. Do you think I'd be able to?"

"Too right you'd be able to, darlin'. Sounds mad I know, but I go back and talk to my plant pot like I'm talking to my ma and da."

"That doesn't sound mad. That sounds lovely."

"Ah well. It gives me a little comfort anyway, and I think we need all the comfort we can get these days, don't you?"

"I'll drink to that," Scotty said, taking another drink from the bottle and offering it to Jules, who put her hands up.

"Nah, better keep my wits about me. God knows I need extra to make up for the three halves my brothers are missing between them," she said, just as Rob was looking perplexed as to why the loaded trolley he was trying to push back out of the room was not moving. She walked across and flicked the two brakes up with her foot then turned to Jon, who had pushed the brakes on in the first place. "We've got a job to do. No larking about."

Jules walked out of the pantry and headed along the corridor to the mess. Natural light shone into the hallway from the propped open double doors. George and Rog stood at the fire exit waiting for the first of the trolleys to arrive. Jules went across to them. "While we're getting the food loaded, we could do with another team unloading the trashed truck if you've got any spare bods," Rog said.

Jules looked towards the army vehicle with its canvas top parked parallel with the pantry. "Everybody else is tied up right at the moment, but I can make a start on that."

"I didn't realise you got your hands dirty; thought you were management," Rog said with a grin.

"You cheeky fuckin' shite, I'll give you management," she said, smiling.

The team worked like a well-oiled machine. As the pantry emptied, more people joined Jules. Eventually, there was no more space in the box van, and it was time for George to take over with the decoy duties that Ben and Olly were carrying out so well. The group had remained vigilant and occasionally heard the odd vehicle horn but had not seen a single creature.

"I don't like you going alone," Jules said, taking hold of George's arm as she walked him to the van.

"It makes sense. The more people helping you load, the sooner you'll be done and it's better if Rog stays here. If anything goes wrong, it will be good to have a trained soldier around."

"Yeah, but what if you run into trouble?"

"Then it's better to just put one old man at risk than two people, isn't it?"

"I was thinking more about the supplies," Jules replied.

"Cheeky bugger. I'm not going to run into trouble, and you're going to need Rog here to show you where everything is."

Suddenly, Andy overtook them without saying a

word and went to sit in the passenger seat of the box van. Jules and George gave each other a confused look. When they reached the van, Jules opened the driver's door and looked across at her brother. "What's going on?"

Andy held up a pistol. "This is a Glock 17," he said, almost as if he was doing a commercial presentation for it. "Rog has told me how to use it. George can't go alone, so I'm going with him."

"I don't want you shooting bloody guns off, that's the last thing we need," Jules replied.

"I'm not an idiot. I've got no thought of using it unless it's an absolute emergency, but if something happens and we're surrounded by twenty-odd of those things what are we going to do?"

Jules couldn't answer. She looked back towards the rest of the group who were now ferrying military clothing out of the building on the same trolleys they had used for the food. "Watch yourselves, the pair of you," she said, turning to Andy and then to George.

There was a look of apprehension, bordering horror and torment, on George's face as he climbed into the cab. He started up the engine and lowered the window. "Get everybody back inside until the other van's back here. It might not be as straightforward as we hope… Could end up with both vans being followed rather than just one."

Jules nodded, and as George levered off the handbrake, she set about ushering everyone back inside the building. She slammed the fire door closed behind them, and the group just stood there, waiting for a signal to announce the all-clear.

Three minutes later, there was the sound of an engine coming to a stop. A door opened and closed, and then they heard three firm knocks on the fire exit. Jules hit the panic bar, and the door swung open. Ben and Olly were standing there with smiles on their faces, and Jules's face lit up too. She gave them both tight embraces and she was about to issue instructions to the rest of the group to get the second van loaded up when two shots rang out, and the blood in her veins suddenly turned to ice.

5

Nobody moved and nobody spoke for what seemed like an eternity but was actually no more than just a few seconds. Jules thought back to the last words her brother had spoken about only using the gun if it was an absolute emergency. "Stay here," she said to the others, closing the emergency exit behind her and heading to the box van.

Ben ran around to the driver side, and Olly climbed into the passenger seats. They were about to set off when Rog banged on the door. "Budge up," he said, opening it and climbing inside.

Olly squeezed up against Jules and Rog shut the door again, planting the butt of his rifle in the footwell. The wheels began to turn on the van and they'd been travelling less than a minute before they saw the other vehicle completely surrounded by a horde of beasts in military uniform battering the sides and front of the cab. None of them turned as Ben pulled on the handbrake. The full attention of the undead mob was focussed on George and Andy.

"Oh dear God!" Jules cried as she watched the rabid creatures thrashing against the other vehicle. There was a loud bang as the glass in the windscreen splintered, then the same thing happened with the passenger window. "They're sitting ducks. What do we do?"

Ben pressed hard on the horn, the sound temporarily drowning out the growls. A number of the beasts looked in the direction of the sound but just as quickly returned their attention to the prey they had trapped just a few inches beyond the glass.

The box van, despite being weighed down with supplies, began to tip from side to side as the agitated hammering from the horde became even more frantic. Before she knew what was happening, Jules suddenly felt less squashed and looked to her left to see Rog had opened the door and jumped down. He raised his rifle and fired. There was an eruption of red that turned to mist in the air, and one of the creatures fell to the ground. He fired again and a second beast fell, then a third.

Half the horde split from the van and began to sprint towards him. Here was a living, breathing, pink-fleshed body out in the open just ready for the plucking. Rog fired again, and another monster fell. As it hit the ground, he climbed back into the box van. "Put your foot down," he commanded, and Ben did as he was told. The engine revved loudly, and the tyres screeched as the van began to speed towards the advancing beasts. The creatures converged but soon spread again as the vehicle smashed through them. Bodies flew in multiple directions; arms swam through the air, legs kicked at nothing. Two of the beasts collided with the bonnet of the box van head-on. Jules cringed as she saw their rib cages crumble. They remained stuck there for a moment before disappearing beneath the wheels.

Ben slammed on the brakes and turned the vehicle in a big U. More of the creatures surrounding George and Andy suddenly broke off and gave chase. "They're following us, they're following us!" Ben shouted excitedly.

"Okay, stop here again," Rog said. This time, when

he opened the door and jumped out, Jules and Olly got out with him.

"Turn her round," Olly barked through the door before slamming it shut. He looked towards Jules. "You shouldn't be out here."

"Why, because I'm a girl?"

"No, because we've got guns and you've just got that," he replied, nodding towards the hatchet in Jules's hand.

The van moved off, and Rog and Olly took aim at two of the half-dozen creatures sprinting towards them. They fired at the same time. One flew backwards, skidding across the tarmac. Olly's bullet entered his target's shoulder. The creature stumbled a little but was soon back to a full sprint. "Shit!" Olly cried.

They both fired again. Again, Olly's bullet strayed while Rog's brought a second beast down. Jules threw a look behind to see the van still manoeuvring. "Shite!" She looked back towards the creatures and saw that even more had broken away from the crowd and were heading in their direction. "Do your best not to shoot me," she said and started to run towards the advancing monsters.

"What the fuck are you doing?" shouted Olly.

Jules felt her heart race as she took the first strides towards the pack of growling beasts. She had to do something. She would not be able to live with herself if anything happened to Andy or George. She veered right and both monstrous groups changed direction immediately, following her like shoals of piranhas tracking a wounded fish. She continued between two antiquated looking, single-storey buildings as shots began to ring out behind her once more. She heard the roar of the engine as Ben turned the other van around, but as she looked back, she could see that the attention of all the beasts was now firmly fixed on her. Andy and George's van was clear now, but what momentary happiness that gave her soon washed away as she realised the creatures were gaining ground.

41

Another shot fired and the lead beast went down. Others stumbled behind it, giving Jules just a moment's respite. She carried on between the two buildings. Now, though, she really was alone. Rog and Olly would be able to pick off the odd pursuer still, but they would not have a clear line of sight of the front-runners, the ones that presented Jules with the greatest threat.

There were more rifle reports, but as Jules rounded the corner she did not look back to see if any more beasts had fallen. It was enough to hear the multiple pounding feet and the excited growls. These hellish monsters were hot on her trail and getting closer all the time. She could almost feel their grasping fingers upon her.

She rounded the next corner but, just then, her boot landed on a thin layer of gravel, sending her skidding and crashing to the floor. Pain spasmed through her as she made contact with the gritty surface, but that was her last consideration as the demonic horde attacked.

6

The first creature was almost on top of her when she suddenly rolled to the side. It landed face down on the tarmac, flattening its nose in a gory explosion. Two shots fired and Jules heard the high-pitched revving of the box van, but as another beast pounced she did not have the time to see what was going on beyond her own terrifying field of vision. She rolled again, and this time the creature managed to skew its body to land on her like some deranged alligator with frantically snapping jaws.

Jules pushed hard, forcing it off her, then swung her hatchet in a wide arc. The blade cracked through the monster's forehead as a third and fourth beast lunged. The small axe was buried too deep for her to pull it out quickly enough, so she shuffled backwards as further shots fired.

The two pouncing beasts collapsed immediately, but the first creature with the flattened nose reached out, catching Jules's ankle. She screamed and booted it hard with her other foot as yet another bullet fired, causing a monster that looked like a giant from a children's story to drop to its knees. More beasts ran into the back of it resulting in a mini pile-up and, Jules kicked the creature that had her in its clutches even harder. The toe of her left foot made contact with its head, and for a moment its hand clenched her ankle even tighter, but then the fingers unfurled momentarily and she pulled free. She shuffled back on her hands, heels and buttocks, finally springing to her feet and turning to run.

Rog and Olly were stood either side of the tarmac passage between the two buildings, but the focus of her attention now was on the box van that was hurtling straight towards her. She could see Ben in the driver seat desperately waving his left arm, urging her to get out of the way. Jules looked back towards the beasts as they started to gather themselves, and she slowed down then finally stopped. There were only thirteen or fourteen left now, and she knew this was the best chance they had to finish them all off. Within a few seconds, they were charging towards her once more.

Jules turned and sprinted towards the box van as it accelerated even more. She turned her head to glimpse the horde closing then pivoted and dived to the side, crashing onto the hard ground and rolling to a heavy stop. She heard the tyres squeal as Ben adjusted the vehicle's direction. Two beasts emerged into her line of sight and began to charge towards her, but heavy thuds drummed into the air as more still were battered by the speeding box van.

More shots sounded from behind her and both creatures making a beeline for Jules stuttered in mid-stride as one bullet disappeared into a neck and another into a chest, but neither beast fell. She climbed to her feet, jarred, bruised and aching. She started to run towards Olly and Rog. The pair fired again, and as the sound of screeching tyres ripped through the air, Jules dared to turn around. The beasts that had been pursuing her were both down. All but one remaining pair of creatures were on the ground in various states of mobility. Even from a distance, Jules could see most had broken limbs and shattered bodies.

The van straightened up as the last two vertical beasts limped towards it. There were two loud smashes as the creatures were batted off the bonnet at speed, leaving gruesome imprints on the white bodywork. The van swerved twice more, rolling over any beasts that looked like they had the slimmest chance of climbing back to their feet, but the danger was over. The vehicle pulled up in front of Jules, and Ben climbed out, running towards her and clutching her in the tightest of embraces. They held each other for a moment and then finally withdrew.

"What the bloody hell were you thinking?" Ben demanded.

"I had to do something; that was George and my brother in that van."

"That was madness. Do you realise how dangerous that was, Jules?"

"Well, considering it was my arse out there, I've got a pretty good idea, yeah."

"You could have been killed just as easily as not."

"Yeah, well, I wasn't, was I?"

"Not for a bloody lack of trying."

"Jules!" Andy shouted and Jules turned her head. She ran towards her brother and he ran to her. He flung his arms around her and kissed her roughly on the cheek.

"Are you alright?" she asked, pulling back and looking at him to make sure he was not hurt.

"I'm fine."

George came up behind Andy and Jules threw her arms around him too. "What happened?"

"Bloody thing stalled; then it wouldn't start again. I think it's the starter motor. If you hadn't shown up when you did, we'd have been in real trouble," George said.

"Yeah, well, that was a close thing all round," Rog said as he walked across to them. "Right, well, after you've got your breath, let's get your van going, get loaded up and get out of here before dark. I really don't want us to be travelling at night if we can help it."

Jules looked towards Ben, but he had already climbed back into the van, he was obviously still angry with her. She started heading back then stopped and looked around. "What is it?" Olly asked.

Jules turned to Rog. "What's to stop us bringing the gang from the Home and Garden Depot here? I mean we can repair the gate, make it secure and there's plenty of space. Surely—"

"They stopped using this place years ago. It was only when the disaster hit that they reopened it, but they soon wished they hadn't. The buildings are disintegrating and are full of asbestos. The pantry is about the only room in the place whose walls aren't painted with toxic mould. If you've got young or old people among you, this is the last place you want to bring them," Rog said.

Jules let out a sigh. "Ah well. It was just a thought."

Rog and George hitched a tow rope to the van with the faulty starter motor, and once they got the engine running, George kept it running. They filled the second van with all the supplies it could carry then carefully stretchered Scotty on board.

The journey back to the Home and Garden Depot was quiet. Ben did not make eye contact with Jules despite her frequent attempts to grab his attention and even after they had unloaded the vans and introduced the newcomers, the tensions did not ease.

George and Jules made Scotty as comfortable as they could in the cash office, but it was not long until the skies began to darken. They both went upstairs to the manager's office and sat down in the well-padded, comfortable armchairs.

"That was some day," George said.

"You can say that again," Jules replied. "I was scared to death I was going to lose you and that idiot brother of mine."

"There was a time there when I thought you were going to lose us too." George took out his pipe and went through his usual rituals with the tobacco before lighting it and taking a few puffs. "He stepped up today did Andy."

"I know. He's an idiot, but his heart's always in the

right place, and I don't suppose you can ever ask any more than that from someone," she said, looking out of the window as the sun continued its descent.

"Ben's not talking to me."

George paused then took the pipe out of his mouth. "He cares for you. It was a big risk you took."

"I know, but I had to do something."

"He'll come around."

"I hope so."

"Trust your elders."

The door opened, and Maggie walked in.

"We were just talking about you," Jules said.

"What were you saying?"

"George was reminding me I had to listen to my elders," Jules said with a cheeky grin.

"Oh, aren't you the funny one. I heard what happened today," Maggie said, perching on the edge of the desk.

"Yeah well, stuff doesn't always go to plan," Jules replied.

"So it would seem. Rog seems like a nice man."

"Yeah, he and Scotty both seem cool."

"You do realise the other one doesn't have long, don't you?"

Jules straightened up in her chair. "What do you mean? I know his legs are broken but I thought—"

"Sepsis. He's got blood poisoning. Have you seen the colour of his legs?"

"I thought that was just really bad bruising," Jules replied.

"Are you sure?" George asked.

"I'm not an expert, but I'm pretty confident that's what it is. My uncle died of it."

"Oh shite!" Jules said. "How long?"

"I don't know, but not long. I'm pretty certain they both know, Rog and Scotty."

"That's a real shame," George said, taking a suck

on his pipe and releasing a long plume of smoke from his lips.

Maggie coughed and waved at the air. "You and that bloody thing. It'll be the death of you … and us."

Jules opened the bottom drawer of the desk and pulled out a bottle and three glasses. She poured good measures into each glass and pushed one towards Maggie and one to George before picking up her own. "To Scotty," she said.

"He's not gone yet," Maggie replied, picking up her glass and taking a drink.

"No, but I wanted to toast something, otherwise it looks like I'm just an alky."

"I think after the day you've had you deserve a drink, don't you?" Maggie said.

"Y'see, that's why I love having you around. Technically, you're just an enabler, but that's what I need right now," Jules said with a smile. All three of them raised their glasses and clinked.

Maggie downed hers in one and then stood up. "Okay, I'm going to do my rounds before I call it a night, make sure everybody's okay."

"Thanks, Mags. I'm just going to stay up here a while," Jules said.

"Aha! Alcohol and avoidance. Two sure-fire routes to a happy life," Maggie said with a smirk.

"I'm guessing you've been talking to Benicio. Well, you can tell him it's not like I had a bloody choice and I didn't see anyone else coming up with any ideas and … and … fuck him!"

"If it's all the same to you, I'll let you pass on that message. Ooh, I've got an idea," she said, pointing to the bottle, "why don't you have a few more of those first? That will really open up the channels for you both to have a meaningful discussion."

Jules smiled and raised her glass. "Yeah, fuck you too."

"A foul-mouthed alcoholic who's quick to anger. Ben's a lucky, lucky man. I'm surprised he's not up here begging to make it up to you right this minute."

"Be careful when you're walking down those steps, old woman, I'd hate for you to have a fall."

Maggie let out another laugh before leaving and closing the door firmly behind her. Jules brought the glass up to her lips and took two big gulps then refilled it. "You want a top-up?"

"Not for me. I'll have this; then I'll get to bed. That was some day."

"Huh. That's one way to describe it," Jules said, taking another gulp.

"Thank you, Jules."

"What for?"

"If you hadn't done what you did, if you hadn't risked your life, I wouldn't be sitting here now. There are a lot of people who would have frozen, who would have been too scared to act, and I wouldn't have blamed them."

"Yeah, well. That's not me. Act first; think later," she said, taking another drink.

"We both know that's not true either. This place is lucky to have you. You always hold yourself to the highest standards. You do that despite your fears, and that's what makes you who you are. You're special, Jules. You remind me of my youngest granddaughter."

Jules smiled. "God, you shouldn't say that about the poor girl. Surely she can't be as big a screw-up as me."

"On the contrary. She's ... she was in the squad for the next commonwealth games. She's only fifteen but she's got that X-factor."

"I hardly think I've got the X-factor."

"I disagree. You do what it takes. I can sometimes see the fear and uncertainty in you for just the briefest of seconds." George took a long drink from his glass, then fixed his eyes back on Jules. "But then you push it down deep inside. You don't want others to see it, to feel it, so you swallow it and make believe everything's okay. That is true heroism. It's not the absence of fear; it's doing the right thing, the hard thing, despite your fear."

"Ah shush!" Jules said.

"You know I'm right."

"Away with you," she said, blushing.

George smiled and finished his whisky, placing the empty glass back down on the table and standing up. "Right, I'll do my own rounds, make sure we're all locked up safe and tight and then get some shut-eye." He walked around the desk, bent down and kissed Jules gently on the top of her head. "Thank you again."

Jules gulped, suddenly overcome with emotion. "Brilliant, my hair's going to smell of fucking whisky and tobacco now. Thank you very much, old man." George smiled and Jules took hold of his hand giving it a tight squeeze. When she spoke again, it was in a softer voice. "I'd be lost without you." They held hands for a few more seconds before Jules relinquished her grip. "Alright, that's the soppy stuff over, you can fuck off now."

George laughed. "Goodnight Jules."

"Sweet dreams."

The room fell silent as George left and Jules drained her glass then refilled it. George knew her too well. She could not remember a time when she had been more scared, and now all that fear was coming to the surface as tears began to roll down her face. The last of the sunlight was just disappearing on the horizon as she contemplated just how close she had come to never seeing another. She swirled the magic amber potion beneath her nose. She had made a real mess of things with Ben. Maybe after the two of them had a good night's sleep, the anger and frustration would have dissipated enough for them to talk.

The door creaked open, and Jules looked towards it. She could just make out Ben's figure in the doorway. "Hi," he said.

"Hi."

"I owe you an apology," he said, walking towards her.

"That's funny; I was just sitting here thinking that I owed you an apology."

She stood up and, as he approached her, their hands reached out and met, fingers entwining. "You scared me today."

"I scared myself. If I'd have thought about it a bit longer, I'd probably have figured something else out, but..."

"I know. I know you had to do something. I suppose I was just angry with myself for not doing something first." Jules tiptoed up and kissed him on the lips. "Is that a single malt?"

Jules let out a small giggle. "You want some?"

"Yeah and I'd like some scotch too."

"Benicio Hernandez, I don't know what kind of girl you think I am, but I have a reputation to uphold."

He reached for the glass on the desk and took a drink. "I know all about your reputation," he said, kissing her on the lips. The light had dipped even further, but he could feel the smile on her face as their mouths met.

"Is the door locked?" Jules asked.

"No."

"Well, go lock it and come straight back," she said, pulling her T-shirt off.

"What about your reputation?" he asked, almost running towards the entrance and locking it.

"Well, y'know there's been like billions of deaths, so procreation is kind of a duty and shit. It's like we're doing this for mankind."

Ben walked back towards her pulling off his own T-shirt and unbuckling his belt. "You are such a martyr."

"Totally. St Jules of Carrickfergus. That's me."

7

The next morning, Jules woke up at first light. The blinds had not been closed the previous evening. She had consumed more than her fair share of scotch but remembered all the important details. She and Ben had made love over and over in the cool embrace of the moonlight's glow. They had forgiven each other, and now, as she rested her head on his shoulder while he slept, she realised that not everything was bad about this world.

She was not in love with Ben. She didn't know if she would ever love him. But she liked him. He was kind and considerate and fun to be around. His good looks and Mediterranean colouring made her heart jump a little every time she saw him, but she knew that was just physical attraction and that was very different to love. She had been in love once, a few years ago. It had ended badly and that's why she had left Belfast and moved across to Scotland. She remembered what love felt like, and this was not that, but it was something, and to have something in this nightmarish time was bordering on a miracle.

She heard someone try the door handle and when it didn't open, they knocked three times. She jumped to her feet wearing nothing but a look of panic. Ben's eyes sprung open. "What's going on?" he asked, still a little groggy from the whisky.

"Jules, are you okay?" It was Maggie.

"Err … yeah, give me a second, Mags." She pulled on her bra and T-shirt as Ben suddenly realised what was happening and began to dress too.

"What did I do with my knickers? Where are my fucking knickers?" Jules whispered desperately.

It was taking Ben all his time to focus on putting his socks on. "Calm down, they'll show up."

Jules cast another panicked look around the floor then pulled on her jeans anyway. She slipped on her socks and boots, opened a window and headed to the door. She paused with her thumb and forefinger on the key then, when Ben gave her the nod, she unlocked the door and opened it.

"Come in, Mags, we were just … err … getting ready to come down."

Maggie stepped into the room and sniffed at the air. "Smells like a distillery in here. Did you have a party last night?"

"It was kind of a stressful day yesterday; we needed to kick back a little."

"I see," Maggie said, stopping dead and staring towards the poster-sized framed photo of the Home and Garden Depot opening ceremony. Jules was a little confused as to why she looked towards it so long and even more confused to see the grin appear on Maggie's face. "Anyway, I'm sorry to disturb both of you so early, but it's Scotty. I'm afraid he's taken a turn for the worse."

"Shite," Jules said. "Okay, we'll be right down."

Maggie placed a gentle hand on Jules's arm and leaned in to whisper something to her before turning to leave. Jules stood perfectly still, but her face turned bright red. When Maggie closed the door behind her, Ben broke the silence. "What's wrong? What did she say?"

Jules looked at Ben but didn't say a word.

Eventually, she turned and walked up to the large photo that Maggie had been looking at. She plucked her knickers from the top left corner of the thick wooden frame and stuffed them in her pocket. "How fuckin' embarrassing!"

Ben laughed. "Come on. Maggie was young once, I'm sure she understands."

Jules just shook her head. "How the fuck did they even get over there?"

"It's coming back to me now. At one stage you flung them behind you saying you wouldn't be needing these again tonight."

"Oh dear God, where's a big hole to swallow you up when you need one?"

"You've got to see the funny side," Ben said.

"Erm, no. No, I don't." The two of them headed out of the room and down to the shop floor. The bays that used to contain lengthy strips of hardwood, plasterboard and a hundred DIY essentials had been converted into curtained cubicles to give the residents within some small modicum of privacy. Many of these curtains were still pulled across indicating the people behind them were either asleep or wanted to be left alone.

They reached the front of the store and Maggie was standing outside the small cash office where they had put Scotty in order to give him as much comfort and dignity as possible. "He was asking for you," Maggie said.

"For me?" Jules replied.

"Yes."

"I'll leave you to it and go get cleaned up," Ben said, giving Jules's hand a gentle squeeze.

Jules looked at the door then looked back towards Maggie. "What does he want to see me for?"

"I don't know. He's a little bit delirious, but he was adamant about seeing you."

Jules took a breath and opened the door. She gagged a little as the smell of necrotic flesh assaulted her senses. Rog was sitting in an office chair by the side of

Scotty's makeshift bed. When Jules entered, he stood up. "It's been a long night. I'm going to stretch my legs and get some air." Sadness painted his expression, and he did not look back at his friend as he left the room. The wide one-way mirror let in enough light from outside for Jules to see that the blackish purple discolouration that she had originally mistaken for bruising had spread up to the lower part of his neck. As Scotty turned his head to look at her, perspiration clung to his brow, and each blink looked like an effort.

"Looks like you've had a rough night, darlin'," Jules said warmly.

A small smile adorned his lips for just a second. "Had better." When he spoke, it was with a rasp and his face contorted as if it caused him pain.

"You wanted to see me?"

He gave a barely perceptible nod then swallowed hard. "I'd like to plant those seeds you talked about. I'd like to plant them for my family."

"Okay. Okay, we can do that. Is there anything else?"

"Not just yet," he whispered.

"Okay, darlin', just give me a couple of minutes and I'll get that sorted." Jules left the office and a tear ran down her face. She had never been asked to grant a dying wish before, and this was most definitely that. She rushed down the end aisle towards the huge enclosed yard. As she pulled the doors open, she looked above the wall, above the chain-link and barbed wire fence mounted on top of it and towards the blue sky. It was going to be another beautiful day but not for everybody.

She walked over to a shelving unit and grabbed a plastic plant pot. She was about to fill it with seed compost when she stopped. At the back of the shelf, there was a head-sized glazed ceramic blue pot. It was one of the more expensive ones the store sold. She put the plastic one to the side and grabbed the posh one instead. Everybody else here had the opportunity to transplant their memorials into whatever they wanted. Scotty would not have that chance, so it was only right that he had the best to start off with. Jules picked up a sheet of sticky labels and a packet of seeds, putting them in her pocket before grabbing the plant pot and transporting it to the cash office.

She headed through the store and heard the first sounds of the morning for some, as the sheets that covered their cubicles began to twitch and flutter while they got dressed. The brief happiness she had enjoyed, at least what she could remember of it, from the previous evening now seemed like it was an age ago.

She opened the cash office door and in her brief absence had forgotten just how pungent the odour had been in the confined space; she did her best not to show it, though, as she knelt by Scotty's side and gently placed the pot down. "Pretty," he whispered.

"Thanks very much, you're not so bad looking yourself," Jules said with a smile.

Scotty couldn't help but smile. "You're a sweet girl, Jules. These people are lucky to have you."

"You're only saying that cos you haven't known me long enough. Give it a couple of weeks and you'll be eating those words."

He smiled again and this time let out a long, long breath. Jules went cold as Scotty's eyes seemed to stare blankly into space for a moment like there was nothing behind them; then he breathed in again. "I'd love to spend that long with you, but I don't think I'm going to have much choice in the matter." He looked towards the plant pot again, just the small turn of his head seeming like the biggest effort. "So how do we do this?"

Jules picked up the packet of seeds and showed him the picture. "These are the ones I planted for my own folks. It's called a Chinese Evergreen," she said. "Now, how many kids did you have?"

"Two," he rasped, holding out his hand. "But I'd

like one for my ex as well."

Jules nodded and tapped three seeds into his palm. She pinched a measure of soil from the plant pot and guided Scotty's hand across to the small hole she had made. He tipped the seeds in then Jules gave him the small clump of compost to place over them. Scotty tapped it down gently and then Jules took the bottle of water sitting next to his pillow and poured a little over where the seeds had been sown. "There, job's a good 'un. Now, what were their names?" Jules asked, taking a pen from the holder on the desk and picking up the sheet of labels.

"Suzy and Garth. My ex was called Bernice." Jules wrote the names on the label, peeled it off the sticker sheet and carefully placed it on the plant pot.

"There we go, darlin'. Do you want to say anything?"

"Like what?"

"Some people say a prayer. Some just say a few words as if they were talking to them. Some say nothing at all."

"Well, I just wish I'd have been there. I wish I'd have been there with them. Been more of a dad and more of a husband. Maybe in the next life, eh?"

Jules placed her hand over his. "We all have regrets. Words that we didn't get the chance to say, but I'm sure they knew you loved them, and, in the end, that's all that counts."

The words gave Scotty some comfort, and he gave Jules's hand a weak squeeze. "Can you do one more thing for me?"

"Course I can."

"When I go, can you plant a seed for me in there? I don't want to spend eternity alone."

Jules's eyes widened as she tried to hold back tears. This was one of the saddest things she'd ever heard. "None of us spends eternity alone, darlin', that's not how it works, but I'll happily plant a seed for you in there too. Let's hope that's not for some time yet, eh?"

Scotty looked at Jules for a long time and she looked back. She did not know what to do to try to comfort him, to alleviate his doubts, so she just remained there kneeling by his side, holding his hand. Eventually, he closed his eyes. "I think I'll try to have a nap."

"You do that. I'll go and place this with the others." Jules picked up the plant pot and walked to the door, throwing one final glance back to the frail-looking figure lying on the floor before heading out.

Rog walked up to her. "Thank you for that."

"You don't need to thank me. He's sleeping now."

"Sleep's good. Hopefully, it will come for him in his sleep and he'll go without too much more suffering."

They carried on walking towards the garden depot. "Is there anyone you want to say goodbye to?"

"Already said my goodbyes. Not much of a believer I'm afraid. I struggle to see how a god could allow all this. I know they say he works in mysterious ways but…"

"But what?"

"I saw a young mother running from those things with her baby in her arms. They caught her and dragged her down. The baby went quiet. Didn't come back, but she did. I was protecting a group of about fifteen school kids and their teacher at the time. There was nothing I could do about it until that woman started running towards us, with half her throat hanging out. I took down the ones that attacked her; then I had to take her down. So if there is a god, mysterious ways or not, fuck him!" Rog said and turned back towards the cash office.

Jules stood there for a moment, the thought of the woman and child sending a shudder through her. She understood Rog's anger and his reluctance to believe, but there had to be more than this. There had to be.

8

"Knock, knock, are you decent?" Jules asked as she stood outside the bay that used to house flatpack children's wardrobes but was now George's living space. The cloth curtain that had once been a dust sheet (aisle three - decorating supplies) opened, revealing a compact living environment that the Japanese would have been proud of.

George had fixed plasterboard to the rear and sides of the space, giving him and his neighbours more privacy. A framed print of New York City at night hung just above where his head would rest on his makeshift corrugated cardboard mattress.

"Take a seat," he said, sitting down on the flattened out boxes.

Jules crouched so as not to bang her head on the shelf above and sat down beside him. At the side of the 'bed', there was a small upturned plastic box. On it sat a torch, a bottle of water and a family photo.

"You never struck me as a New York type," Jules said, nodding towards the poster.

"No ... no, can't say I am. I saw it, and it made me smile. It's just a reminder."

"A reminder of what?"

"My eldest granddaughter, Robyn. She really wanted to go to New York. I think it was ever since watching that *Miracle on 34th Street*. You know; the Christmas film. She wanted to see the parades; she wanted to go to the shops. I told her one day I'd take her. I don't suppose I'm going to get to keep that promise now, but I saw this picture, and it just made me think of her."

"That's nice," Jules said, looking at the picture. "So, what's on the to-do list today?"

"Well, I was thinking. The road out of town was pretty quiet when we were travelling yesterday. We passed a couple of service stations and a big boarding school."

"And?"

"Well. There'll be all sorts we can use from both … before anybody else gets to them first."

"Okay, the petrol stations I can understand, but what are we going to find at a school?"

George let out a sigh. "What do they have in schools?"

"Books."

"Who reads the books?"

"Kids?"

"Now, I realise you're not a parent, but one commonality between all children is they need food. At a boarding school, that's breakfast, lunch and dinner, and they're not going to be buying a tin at a time. These places get the best deals by buying in bulk. Everything happened so quickly that there's a good chance the food could still be there. What's more, if it looks safe enough, it might be an option for us … to move everyone out of the city."

Jules sat back, her shoulders rested against the plasterboard wall. She looked across the aisle to the opaque plastic sheeting covering another makeshift bedsit. A figure began to stir within. "I suppose it couldn't be any worse than this place. But it's a big operation moving everybody from here, all our stuff."

"If we don't do it soon, we'll never do it."

"How do you mean?"

"Well, think about it. We're finding new people in the city all the time, some of them not in the best state. The more of us there are, the harder it will be. The fuel won't last forever and even though we're on the outskirts, we're still in an area with a population of over forty thousand. The food we got yesterday was a real bonus, it's given us a breathing space, but it won't last forever. And look at this place," George said, gesturing up and down the aisle. "Do you really want to live here?"

"I hadn't really thought about us living here, it was just…"

"A stopgap?"

"Well, yeah."

"That time's been and gone, what are we waiting for?"

"We've got old people. We've got a pregnant woman, we've got sick, we've got—"

"That's what I'm saying. We've delayed moving, and we've even started turning this place into a kind of shantytown, but that school … it could be just what we're looking for."

"This is why you should be in charge. I can't think like you."

"No thanks. I'm more of a behind-the-scenes type."

"Okay, I'll get a group together; we'll go check it out. I assume you're my first volunteer."

"I have a choice? I thought I was your majesty's chauffeur."

"I'll majesty you, you sarky old bastard."

George smiled before turning more serious. "I'm assuming Rog will be staying here."

"I'd have thought so, but I'll ask him. We'll head out after breakfast."

*

George was in the lead vehicle as they drove out of

61

town. Jules and Ben were in the two passenger seats. There was another box van and a transit behind.

"I really didn't expect Rog to be coming," Ben said, looking into the wing mirror.

"It's not an easy thing to watch a friend die," George said.

"No, I suppose not."

Ben had a rifle clamped between his knees. "You sure you know how to use that?" Jules asked.

Olly's been giving me training. "We've got plenty of guns but hardly any ammunition, but he said it's good that we get used to them; then, when we do find an ammo store, we'll know what we're doing."

"Great so we're going to have a bunch of gung-ho halfwits running around shooting at shadows. Remind me to thank him, will you?"

Ben smiled. "So I'm a gung-ho halfwit?"

"When you point that thing, just make sure it's not in my direction," Jules replied.

"Your confidence in me is overwhelming."

"Yeah well, no offence, but growing up with three brothers, I know just what men are like when they've got a new toy."

"No disrespect, but I think your brothers are special cases," Ben replied.

"Yeah, can't argue with that, I suppose."

"I think we've got a bit of a weather front coming," George said, looking towards the black clouds to the left.

"Where the hell did they come from? It was sunny five minutes ago," Jules replied.

"This is Scotland, remember. You can get four seasons in a day. Still, that's not a bad thing. I just hope Maggie has the sense to get some buckets out in the garden section."

"She will. Mags will always keep things running right when we're not there."

They carried on for a few more minutes; then the

first raindrops began to lash against the windscreen. A sombre greyness shrouded the vehicle and the landscape and, for the time being anyway, all thoughts of summer disappeared in a deluge. Accompanying the rain was a gusting, wind and just the appearance of the inclement weather made them all feel cold.

The fields gave way to a tall, red brick wall enclosing woodland, and George began to slow the box van. He placed the left indicator on and turned. The wall continued on both sides of the road for a moment until it reached a pair of imposing black wrought-iron gates. He pulled on the handbrake and climbed out. The rain tore at his face as he braved the few feet to unlatch the sturdy barrier and push the gates inward. He walked back to the van, climbed in and shivered. "I think we should have brought our big coats. It's going to be a wet one."

"Well, if this place is all you think it is, it'll be worth it," Jules said as George pulled off the handbrake and the convoy began to roll on. Jules looked at the well-polished brass nameplate by the side of the road. *St. Chad's school for boys.* The wall ended and the road was lined on either side with trees as they drove up the long winding track. It eventually widened into a vast gravel courtyard and there stood the magnificent Victorian building in all its splendour. "Jesus! How the other half lives ... lived."

The building was vast. Hundreds of windows looked out over the courtyard. To the left, there was a rugby field with a football field beyond that. To the right, there was a road with a sign saying, *Deliveries.* "So where do we start?" Ben asked.

"Well, I'm guessing the kitchen is going to be around the back, so that sounds like a good place to me," George replied, following the *Deliveries* sign. Jules and Ben just gawped as the van drove along the full length of the impressive structure.

"Can you imagine the heating bill?" Ben said.

"Well, that's one of the reasons I wanted to check

this place out. I'm guessing it's got its own furnace. I'm guessing it's got a lot of things. If there was a power cut, you couldn't have all those children of privilege roughing it. I'm sure there are all sorts of redundancies here," George said.

"Smart thinking," Ben replied.

"I have my moments," George said, turning a corner and bringing the van to a stop in a spacious tree-lined car park. The flaying rain was not as harsh here as the building and the trees shielded the vehicles from the worst of the weather. Everybody climbed out of the vehicles and gathered together around Jules. George walked up to a pair of wide, dark oak doors. There was a bell button by the side of it with a small sign saying, *Please ring for attention*. George pressed it, but there was no accompanying chime. He knocked hard against the wood.

"What the hell are you doing that for?" Jules asked.

"You never know. There might be someone at home," George replied. The knock went unanswered, and he tried the door, but it was locked.

Olly stepped forward with a long crowbar and wedged the thin edge into the narrow gap where the two doors met. Small splinters of wood chipped away as he levered the cold black metal from side to side. He forced the bar in further and pulled harder and finally a loud crack burst through the sound of the wind and rain. The door on the right swung inwards slowly revealing a sizable and well-equipped kitchen with a black-and-white tiled floor that looked like it belonged in a top London restaurant rather than a school.

The group filtered through the entrance, leaving the cold wind and rain behind. Not a single pot or pan was out of place. "This kitchen is bigger than the assembly hall at my old school," Jules said.

"It's bigger than my old school," George replied.

They advanced down the centre aisle towards a painted white door. "I'm guessing that's the pantry," Jules said.

"Only one way to find out," Ben replied, opening it. It was dark inside, and he flicked on a torch. "Holy crap," he said as the beam panned around. The room was around thirty feet by twenty feet; it made the pantry they had found at the barracks look like a small tuckshop.

"This will keep us going for months," Jules said, turning on her own torch and walking inside. She looked at the food on the shelves. The tins were all big-name brands. "No cheap generic shite for this lot."

"The fees for this place will have been thousands per term. They're not exactly going to have to buy Aldi's own-brand baked beans to make ends meet, are they?" George said as they headed back into the light of the kitchen.

"Right, so what's the plan?" Rog asked, looking towards Jules.

Jules looked around at the assembled faces. "There are sixteen of us. If we all go around together, it'll probably take us a week to check this place out. We'll split up into groups of four. Rog, you lead one group. Olly, you lead another. Ben, you take another group. We'll start on this floor; then, when we're happy it's clear, we'll head upstairs."

"Okay, so how do we this?" Olly asked.

"A room at a time. We need to clear it in sections and not separate out too much. We don't want anybody getting stranded if there are some nasty surprises lurking anywhere. Everybody be careful. The place looks empty, but you never know."

Rog and Olly began to divide the group up into smaller teams, but Ben sidled up to Jules, gently guiding her to one side. "I don't like the idea of you being in the only group without a rifle."

"We've all got weapons. We've managed so far without guns, we can manage now and, trust me, if we run into trouble, I'm not exactly the shy, retiring type. You and everybody else in this building will know about it."

Ben smiled. "Yeah, I suppose you're right." He

looked around the fixtures and fittings. "This place could be just what we're looking for. It could be somewhere to build a future."

"I know," Jules replied, "a comfortable future at that. I mean, can you imagine what the dorm rooms are like? These rich little fuckers will hardly have been slumming it, will they?"

Ben smiled. "You have such a way with words."

"Funny, George said the same thing."

"It must be true then," Ben replied.

They both shared a smile before Jules clapped her hands. "Okay, everybody knows what they're doing, let's get to work."

Ben, Olly and Rog all led their teams out of the internal kitchen doors leaving Jules, George, Ellen and Justin in the huge kitchen. "Hang on a second," Justin said, looking at the unimpressive knife he brandished as a weapon. He walked over to the far end of the kitchen and pulled a shining meat cleaver from a magnetic rack on the wall. "Yeah, much better."

"Actually, that's not a bad idea," Ellen said, placing her own knife down on the counter and grabbing a much longer, sharper-looking one from the same rack.

Jules looked at the crowbar she held, gauging the weight of it in her hand; she was more than happy with her choice of weapon. "Come on then, let's get to work."

They left the kitchen and, despite there being no lights on in the long hallway, enough natural light bled in from the many windows for them to be able to see what they were doing. Rog's and Olly's teams were assembled outside two rooms; Ben's team had already entered the first classroom in the left corridor.

Jules watched as Rog knocked on the thick wooden door. She realised he was the only one who really knew what he was doing. He would have probably done this a dozen times before. He should be leading this mission; he should be leading the group. Maybe soon. Maybe, after he'd settled in a little and got over the impending trauma of his friend's death then, he could take over from her. That would be good … better than good. The group would have someone who wasn't just guessing and hoping all the time. They would have a leader with experience and abilities.

Rog waited for a few seconds; then, when he was sure there were no charging feet or hellish growls, he pushed the door open and entered the room. The rest of his squad followed. Jules noticed that Olly had been watching him too. He copied Rog's actions at the entrance he was standing at; then it was down to Jules. She walked up to the next door in the hallway and tapped on the wood with the end of her crowbar. She waited for a few seconds and then opened the door.

It was a classroom with just a handful of desks and chairs. Jules looked out of the window to a giant square courtyard. The entire school was built around what was once a beautifully kept lawn. The grass was a little overgrown now, but she could imagine the pupils out there at break times and on hot summer afternoons. "This place really was something else."

"It still is," George said. "This could be all ours. There's no reason we can't move everybody out here, Jules. It's already not far off being a fortress. We could reinforce the gate, we'd be out of the city; it would be perfect."

Jules turned towards him. "We could plant crops," she said in an almost dream-like way.

"Never mind just planting crops. We've got greenhouses and polytunnel kits back at the Depot. Look at the square out there. It's almost blowing a gale, but barely a blade of grass is moving. It's perfect; we wouldn't have to worry about our food supply being wiped out by a bad storm. This place has got everything we need."

Jules broke into a smile. "I don't think I've ever seen you as excited as this."

"Don't you realise what this place is, Jules? It's the answer to all our problems."

9

She looked back out to the square as the rain continued to fall and the smile on her face broadened. George was right; this place could give them all a new start. "And I suppose there are enough trees around to cut for firewood too."

Now it was George's turn to smile. "That's just what I was thinking." There was a knock on a door further down the hall as one of the other groups continued their search of the premises. "Come on; let's check the rest of this place out."

It took them half an hour to clear the ground floor; then they climbed the grand staircase and began their search of the upper level. The dorm rooms were impeccably decorated with only the finest furnishings. The odd poster adorned the walls to give them a more homely feel. All of the rooms had plenty of natural light, and in each room, there were four alcoves with a bed, desk, chest of drawers and wardrobe in each. The rooms were en suite and Jules could tell that she and George were not the only ones who were getting excited by the prospect of moving into the place.

Ellen brushed her hand over a Spider-Man quilt. "I

bought one of these for my nephew," she said as her fingers suddenly clenched the material. "Spider-Man, Spider-Man, Spider-Man, that was all he ever talked about." A look of melancholy swept over her face.

Jules walked up to her and took hold of her other hand. "Your sister and her family might be somewhere now thinking that they've lost you. Nothing's a fact until it's a fact."

Ellen turned towards Jules and was about to respond harshly, but then she saw nothing but sincerity in her friend's eyes. "You're right. It's just…"

"Hard," Jules finished her thought. "I know exactly how you feel. We all do. We've all lost people, but we've found each other, and what's to say that the same thing hasn't happened for our loved ones? What's to say your sister and your nephew aren't with a group like us, trying to find their way? Things won't be this way forever, Ellen. Six months … a year from now, things could be very different. What we need to do is survive … build a life, a future. We already have a community and a place like this will give us the chance to thrive, get bigger, and, who knows, one day we might be reunited with the ones we've lost."

"Do you really believe that?"

"You should know me well enough by now. I don't take bullshit, and I don't dish it out. Yes, I believe that."

Ellen squeezed Jules's hand tighter. "Thank you."

"You don't have to thank me. We look out for each other. That's what we do."

"Come on," called Justin from the doorway. "We're way behind the others." The mood became more and more buoyant as the four groups proceeded down the long corridor and turned onto the next. From the thick blue carpet with the school's insignia printed into the design to the portraits of famous alumni that adorned the walls, everything about the place suggested opulence. The knowledge that this could soon be their home gave all of them a sense of excitement.

"No fucking way!" Olly said as his group, and then Rog's stopped outside a set of double doors. Ben and Jules's teams caught up and they all stood back to look at the framed posters on either side.

THIS WEEKEND
A WORLD WAR II DOUBLE BILL
SCHINDLER'S LIST
DUNKIRK

"They've got their own fucking cinema?" Jules said, barely believing her eyes.

Rog stepped up to the door and banged on it with the palm of his hand. He waited a few seconds and when there was no sign of life, he pushed the doors open. Beyond it was pitch black and he immediately flicked on his torch. Olly switched his on too, and they stepped inside. There was a small foyer with a popcorn machine and a poster behind reading:

ST. CHAD'S CINEMA CLUB
RECRUITING NOW
CONTACT MR WELLS FOR INFO

The foyer split into two corridors, one to the left and one to the right. Signs, once illuminated, now just relics, pointed to ALL ROWS SEATS 1 – 15 and ALL ROWS SEATS 16 – 30.

"You and Olly head that way," Rog said, looking towards Ben, "Jules and I will go this way."

"Okay," Ben said, "first round of snacks is on me." He smiled.

The two groups separated and more torch lights turned on as they made their way down the narrow passageways. Classic movie posters hung on the walls, and Jules kept looking towards George and the others as their faces expressed the same wonderment she was feeling. *This place was a dream.* Then, just like in a dream, everything began to feel a little cloudy, a little surreal.

Rog tapped hard on the thick wooden door with the butt of his rifle and, at the same instant, a chilling cry macheted through the darkness. Everyone froze to the spot for a moment as the very marrow in their bones turned to ice. More terrified screams erupted and now their soaring wails had an all too familiar accompaniment as growls resonated through the corridor.

Suddenly a hundred feet could be heard thundering down the steps from within the cinema. The looks of wonderment that had been on the group's faces just a few seconds earlier had now changed to expressions of terror as the reality of the situation enveloped them.

"Back! Get back now!" Rog shouted, pushing through the others and leading the charge back down the corridor. He ran around the corner to see Ben standing in the entrance. He was covered in blood and Rog brought his rifle up ready to shoot him, believing he had already turned, but Ben threw his hands up.

"It's me," was all he managed as the screams continued to ring out. He turned back towards the left corridor hoping to see more of his team emerging, but all that came were despairing howls.

"Where's your weapon?" Rog demanded.

"I dropped it."

"Where is everybody?" Jules demanded as she and the others joined Rog and Ben.

Rog looked towards Ben and he knew in that instant that the younger man had no idea. He had seen it before with dozens of comrades. In most cases of fight or flight, people's survival instincts would choose flight. "Come on, we need to get these doors shut," he said, grabbing Ben by the arm and forcing him into the outer corridor. The others followed, but Jules remained in the foyer looking down the dark passage towards the sound of her screaming friends.

"Olly, Max, Sara?" she said almost to herself as she stared into the darkness.

George ran back into the foyer and grabbed her. "They're gone, come on, we need to get out of here." He started pulling her towards the exit when the first creature emerged from around the corner. It looked disoriented at first, but then its eyes focused on the two fresh pieces of meat tussling in the entrance.

Jules's mouth fell open. "Oh my God! It's Olly," was all she could whisper as tears began to fall down her cheeks.

The creature, though, was not Olly. Olly no longer existed. The thing that rushed towards Jules from the darkness was a beast of pure malevolence. It was not the man who had playfully flirted with her when they had first met. It was not the man who had bravely brought in stragglers from the outskirts of the city and volunteered for every scavenger mission going. It was now a monster … a creature of hate intent on swelling the ranks of its species.

It launched at Jules like a missile, its strange grey fingers stretching towards her as it flew. Jules could not move. She tried but she couldn't. Even as George attempted to drag her, she felt as though she was cemented to the spot. It was only when something blurred in her field of vision that she woke to what was actually happening.

Rog shoulder barged the Olly-beast and it went crashing into the popcorn machine, making a din that drowned out all the other sounds in the cinema. The momentum nearly proved too much for Rog, and he almost fell over, but he managed to gather himself just in time. "Move! Now!" he shouted towards Jules and George, and this time Jules did move.

She ran out of the main entrance into the wide, well-lit corridor. She looked towards Ben and gasped as the full horror of seeing him covered in blood from head to foot hit her. She glanced back towards the doors as Rog desperately tried to close them once more. The mechanism was slow and it required patience, but that was a luxury they could not afford. Justin went to help him, but before they could even get the first door shut, half a dozen beasts burst through, knocking Justin and Rog to the floor. The rest of the group watched dumbfounded for a few seconds as four creatures pounced on the two fallen men, ripping bloody chunks from their necks and faces.

Jules's was shaking; her tears were still flowing, but as she screamed the words, "Run! Run! Run!" everyone did.

10

They did not look back as they tore down the corridor. They had seen at least two beasts heading after them, but they could hear many more as growls and pounding feet filled the wide hallway. Tears continued to pour down Jules's face as Justin's agonised shrieks ripped through the air.

Another terrified scream sounded, and Jules turned to see Ellen dragged down to the ground by the grasping hands of three beasts, all catching her at once. Beyond her were dozens of creatures charging towards them and even more storming out of the cinema. All notions of this place being their new safe haven were gone now as the only thoughts became about escape and survival.

Jules slowed as she watched the horrifying attack on Ellen and her friend's pleading eyes as first one monster then another sank their teeth into her. Jules felt someone grab her arm, but she shook it free. There was no way they would all outrun these creatures, she needed to do something; after all, this was her fault. She was the one who made the decisions, she had brought everyone here. She turned her head back to the direction of travel and started sprinting once more. They had come here sixteen strong and they had lost ten in the blink of an eye.

Ben led the group around the corner as Jules brought up the rear. They bounded towards the staircase at the end of the hallway as pure terror continued to drive them all as fast as their feet could carry them. The howls of pain had stopped for the time being; as thundering feet and animalistic growls filled the grand corridor Jules knew that the last screams had not yet been heard.

She could almost feel the reaching fingers pulling at the cloth of her shirt as the fleeing group approached the mouth of the wide staircase. There had been awe in her eyes when they had climbed these steps but now she knew this building was no different to thousands ... millions of others worldwide. For all its grandeur, for all its luxurious decor and furnishings, it was nothing but a fancy tomb.

Ben nearly lost his balance as he leapt from the top step. Jules could see George was tiring and there was no way that they could get down these stairs then back through the building to the waiting vehicles before being caught. This was it, this was her one opportunity. Jules watched her five friends negotiate the first few stairs then turned, backing down the top two steps herself and trying to maintain her composure as the marauding army of the undead came towards her.

Two beasts were leading the charge, and as she heard Ben cry her name from the halfway landing, she swung the long crowbar like a baseball bat towards their feet. That was it—her one gambit. The monstrous pair collapsed, their momentum still forcing them in Jules's direction. She turned back around knowing only too well it was just inches that separated them now and her gamble would either buy them time or bring her death that much closer.

She launched herself from the step; her friends had already disappeared down the second flight. She spread her arms out like a bird, how she wished she could fly right now, but flying was not her intention, she was going to hit the

75

halfway landing hard and if she stood any chance of this plan working, she could not afford to lose her balance. Before Jules's feet touched the carpet, the sound she had silently prayed for erupted from behind her. Her boots finally found a solid surface, but it was not the smooth landing she had hoped for.

The speed, height and force of her jump caused her to crash into the wall beneath the wide window. She prepared herself though and bounced back to her feet just in time to see the forward domino motion of the cascading beasts as they toppled over the two creatures she had brought down with the crowbar. Monsters were monsters and when they had chased her from the cinema she had only been concerned with escape, she had never even thought about who these ghoulish creatures had been in life, but now a wave of sadness hit her as she saw the toppling figures and realised these were the pupils of this school. Juniors and seniors alike they were just children whose lives had not even started.

She was dragged back from her thoughts as the first tumbling bodies came towards her like giant snowballs gathering pace down a mountainside. Jules descended the second flight of stairs with more control this time, an ankle injury or a stupid trip would still mean the end for her despite the fact she had bought the group a little time.

George was bringing up the rear of the group and he glanced back. His normally stoic features were contorted into a look of tortured anguish, but then he saw Jules and despite them all still being in mortal danger, relief swept over him. He slowed down and beckoned her to catch up. "Run! Don't wait, run!" she shouted.

George did as she commanded, and Jules gradually gained on the rest of the group until she had caught up. In between laboured breaths George gasped, "I thought I'd lost you," and in that second Jules wanted to cry again. There were a hundred ways he could have said it but those five words made everything she had risked to save the rest of the group worthwhile.

"Don't celebrate yet, old man, we're not exactly out of the woods."

They were fifty metres down the corridor when the drumming feet of an army began to reverberate once more. Jules turned her head to see the creatures storming towards them. The group had a decent lead for the time being, but she could tell George and at least two of the others were starting to feel the effects of the chase. "What are you doing?" George asked as Jules began to slow again.

"I'm right behind you. Keep going and get those bloody vans started," she said. Stopping by the side of a tall trophy cabinet, she tipped it over, causing the glass to smash and wood to splinter. She ran a little farther and there was a heavy wooden bench outside of an office. She dragged it round, so it was at a ninety-degree angle with the wall. The measures would not hinder the creatures too much, but it might give the group the few seconds they needed.

Jules carried on running, and her heart lifted as she saw the kitchen doors swinging open as Ben burst through. She threw another look over her shoulder as the first beasts vaulted over the toppled cabinet. Others stumbled and more still negotiated their way around. The bench proved to be a more successful barrier, though. The first three creatures hurdled it with little effort, but the second wave ploughed into it, stumbling and falling, causing others to do the same.

Jules turned her head back towards the kitchen doors and ran faster than ever now. She stormed through and sprinted towards the open back door, pulling trolleys into the gangway as she went, desperate to give herself and her friends every second, every micro-second. She felt the rush of cold air and rain against her face as the sound of the internal doors being barged open resonated behind her.

Two of the vehicles were already moving away, but George had turned the box van around and opened the passenger door in readiness for her escape. He leaned across, pushing it as the wind fought against him to close it. The tortured expression Jules had seen on his face earlier returned as he looked beyond his friend to the doorway and the emerging beasts. "Run!" he shouted.

"What the fuck do you think I'm doing?" she cried as her feet skidded on the gravel of the courtyard. "Get the fucking wheels moving," she said as she dived towards the open door, sinking her fingers into the upholstery of the seat.

George pulled back, engaged first gear and started turning the wheel as Jules's legs continued to dangle out of the van. His left hand grabbed her jacket and pulled hard before he returned it to the steering wheel. "Are you—"

"Aaarrrggghhh!" Jules screamed as she felt a hand clamp around her calf. "Faster, drive faster," she said, turning her head to see what had grabbed her. A tall creature, probably a senior, had one hand around her leg as it ran, desperately trying to keep up with the increasing speed of the van. The other two beasts lingered behind it, ready to take its place should it fail in its mission to drag her out. Jules pulled her other leg back and kicked hard three times. The third strike was to the side of the beast's head and for the briefest moment it was stunned, but that moment was all that Jules needed. She wrenched her leg free, shuffled up onto the seat and slammed the door shut while the three creatures continued to run by the side of the vehicle like zombie secret service agents keeping up with the president's motorcade.

George straightened the wheel and put his foot down, quickly working through the gears. The beasts began to fall behind, and as he and Jules looked in the wing mirror to see the rest of the undead army storming out of the doorway, they both breathed audible sighs of relief. Soon, the chasing horde had disappeared from view. The van slowed as it drove through the tall, black wrought-iron gates. George stopped the vehicle and jumped out, swinging the gates closed before latching them firmly together.

He climbed back into the van and, as happy as they both were to have escaped, as happy as they both were to know that the other was safe, there was a deep sadness that cradled them. This had been the single worst loss they had ever suffered.

Jules kept her eyes on the road. The other two vans were nowhere in sight. There was a part of her that understood that, but there was another part of her that was deeply disappointed. George had been the only one who had stayed back to make sure she escaped.

Sensing her sadness, George reached his hand across to Jules. She took it gratefully. "This wasn't your fault, Jules."

"How do you figure that? I'm meant to be the leader of this group and I've just led ten of them to their slaughter."

"You know and I know that's not what happened."

"Ten people," she said again, under her breath.

"Funny, I never had you pegged as someone who had a God complex. You are not in control of everything; you are not responsible for everything. I mean it was my bloody idea to head there in the first place, so you could say that I'm the one to blame."

"That's just stupid!"

"No more stupid than what you're saying. Listen to me, Jules, there's always a danger when we head out and today…" George did not need to speak the words; they both knew what today was.

Jules began to cry again. "I never wanted this. I never wanted this responsibility."

"I know you didn't, love, but we rarely get what we want in this life."

11

The news of what had happened had beaten Jules and George back to the Home and Garden Depot. They made their way through the throng of people who had gathered at the front of the store. Momentary happiness swept over the crowd to see the two of them had made it back safely, but it was just that … momentary, as the far greater sadness and realisation that ten of their number were not coming back hit them like a bullet train.

Jules embraced her brothers and Maggie tightly. She squeezed the hands of others and looked but could not see Ben anywhere. George's words echoed in her head, *We rarely get what we want in this life*. She stepped to the front and as much as she just wanted to curl up into a ball and hibernate for the next few months until there was some sign of this apocalyptic disaster coming to an end one way or another, she knew she had to be responsible. She had to do what was expected of a leader.

"Looking around at your faces I can see that you've already heard what's happened." She let out a long breath. "When we set out this morning, I was convinced it was a risk worth taking. But we lost ten people today, ten good people and no risk is worth that. I wanted to come back with good news for you. I wanted to be able to tell you that we'd found a new place to live … a safe place where we could plant crops and stay warm in winter. I was so close to delivering that news to you as well, but then something went wrong and what happened happened, and now we're back here minus friends and with nothing to show for our trouble but three fuel tanks that are a little bit emptier than when we left." Jules paused and looked around at the faces once again. "Anyway, I'm sorry… That's what I really wanted to say, I'm sorry." She did not wait for anybody else to say anything; she turned around and headed towards the door with the sign on that said, "Staff Only."

Jules flicked her torch on and walked up the stairs. She entered the office … her office, slumped down on the chair behind her desk and just stared out of the window as the rain and wind swept in waves against the glass. The never-ending grey sky that stretched out in front of her was their future—harsh, cold, unrelenting. She could feel tears welling again, but what was the point of crying? If she was to cry for everything that made her sad, she would have to shed nearly seven billion tears.

This was life now. She looked at her hands resting on the arms of the chair then at the uniform they had plundered in the raid on the barracks the day before. Who did she think she was? Dressing like an army recruit did not make her a soldier. Rog was a soldier, he was dead. Olly, Justin and Ellen had been conscripts. They were dead. There were two more conscripts in their ranks, and they were just that, conscripts. They had no will to be soldiers; they took no part in the missions, no part in anything other than the bare minimum they needed to do to stay a part of the group.

There was a gentle knock at the door, it was Ben. "I want to be alone," she said as he popped his head around the corner.

"There's something I need to tell you."

Jules did not look at him; she fixed her gaze back out of the window. "Am I speaking Swahili? I said I wanted to be—"

"It was my fault."

The room fell silent for a full minute. "What do you mean?" Jules asked eventually.

Ben took a deep breath. "I mean I was sure there was nothing in that theatre. I mean we'd been making noise all over the place, if anything had been inside, we should have heard it long before opening the door. I got overconfident and I just barged in. They came out of nowhere. Olly was down in a heartbeat, they got him in the doorway and that's what wedged the door open. Then they just came flooding out. I jumped back and fell against the wall while more of us were attacked. It was a pure fluke that I got out of there."

Jules just stared at him in disbelief. "What do you want me to say?"

"I don't know. I just needed to tell you. It wasn't your fault, it was mine."

"It didn't occur to you that a fucking cinema would be soundproofed?"

"No."

"And why was the only person waiting for me when I got out of that place George? Why weren't you there?"

"I screwed up, Jules."

"Screwed up? Is that what you call it?"

"I'm sorry."

"You're sorry?"

"Yes."

"Oh, well, that's alright then. Ten of our fucking friends have been turned into flesh-eating zombies because you fucked up so monumentally, but you being sorry makes everything better."

"I just needed you to know it wasn't you."

"Yeah, thanks for that, I feel a lot better. Now get out of my fucking sight."

Ben did not say another word, he disappeared as quickly as he had appeared and Jules turned towards the window again. She did not know how long she had been sitting there before another knock came on the door. She looked towards it as it opened. It was Maggie.

"You okay, blossom?" she asked.

Jules stared at her. "I don't think I'll ever be okay again."

Maggie walked across and leaned on the desk. The two friends looked at each other. "Have you still got some of that whisky?"

"I'm worried if I start drinking right now, I won't stop."

"Ben came clean downstairs. He told everybody what had happened."

Jules's eyes widened. "What did they say?"

"They didn't get the chance to say anything. George marched up to him and punched him. Everybody was so taken aback they were just stunned into silence. I think Ben was actually grateful. I think he felt he deserved it and more besides."

"Did George say anything?"

"He said, 'Your mistake cost people their lives and that girl up there has been blaming herself for this. Shame on you.' Then he walked off."

Jules opened the bottom drawer and brought out the whisky and two glasses. She poured a measure into each and then pushed one over the table towards Maggie. "You'd think he was my grandad," she said with an appreciative smile.

"Nobody blames you for this, Jules. Really, nobody blames Ben either. Out there, bad stuff happens. Yes, he should have checked the door, but it was stupidity, a momentary lapse of judgement. How many times has Ben been there for us when we've needed him?"

Jules took a sip of her drink. "I suppose you're right."

"I'm afraid I've got some more bad news to add to your day."

"Course you have. Go on."

"Scotty passed away this morning."

Jules's expression barely changed. "I suppose that isn't really a surprise to anyone. Poor guy. Well, at least he's got Rog to keep him company."

"We wrapped the body in plastic and put it in the back of one of the vans. Next time we go out, we'll get rid of it."

"Not exactly a dignified burial, is it?"

"There's not a lot of dignity in anything these days."

"True enough," Jules said, taking another drink. "Did anything else happen while we were out?"

Maggie pulled up a chair and sat, down reaching for the glass and taking a swig herself. "We took in some more refugees."

"What? You went out?"

"No, we spotted them. A family. They came all the way into the car park. They broke into the security box, trying to see if there was any food. They hadn't eaten in days. The father looked like a stick insect."

"Oh well, they've had a lovely welcome, haven't they? Poor bastards."

"They're just grateful not to be out there anymore. They seem like nice people. He was a banker, she worked in human resources."

"That'll be handy," Jules said with no hint of a smile.

"They've survived this long out there. That's something."

"I suppose," Jules said, taking another drink.

"I'm guessing you know why I've come up here."

"Because I'm always such riveting company?"

"Well, there's that. But people need to see you down there. They need to see that you're not giving up."

"That's why I've come up here, Mags. All I want to

do right now is give up. Why don't you and George take over? People like you. People trust you. You've got sensible heads on your shoulders."

"People never see themselves as others see them. You're special, Jules."

Jules leaned forward, placing both her elbows on the desk. "No, I'm really not."

"Yes, you are. There's just something about you that gives people hope. Even when things turn to crap, you give them something to live for."

"I don't want to be that person, Mags. I never wanted to be that person."

"We don't always get what we want in life, do we? So finish your drink, stop feeling sorry for yourself and get your head back in the game."

"Wow! You are so good at motivational speeches … not."

Maggie smiled just as another knock came on the door. George walked in. "Am I interrupting something?"

Jules pulled another glass out from the bottom drawer and placed it on the table. "Maggie was just motivating me."

"Yeah, can't say I'm surprised you need the whisky for that," George said drily.

"I wish I had some ice for your knuckles."

George looked embarrassed. "I think I went a little too far, it's just … never mind."

"It's just what?" Jules asked, sliding the drink across to him.

"Nobody works as hard for this place as you. Nobody suffers the defeats here as much as you and nobody shares the losses here as much as you. People not being accountable for what they've done is one of my bugbears and for him not to stand up … it just…"

Jules could see the frustration on George's face and as he reached for the glass, she placed her hand over his and squeezed gently. "Thanks, old man. I really appreciate it."

"Yes, well, I dare say I'll apologise to him later, but right then, right there, my temper got the better of me." He picked up the glass and took a drink. "What we did today went badly, but it was the right thing to do."

"Went badly? Jesus, that's like saying the *Titanic* ran into a snowflake. It went absofuckinglutely catastrophically."

"Okay, but it was still the right thing to do and I think that we should form a plan, a proper plan I mean."

Jules drained her glass and refilled it then sat back in her chair. "Okay, I'll take the bait, a plan for what?"

"For getting out of this place while we've still got some fuel and a least a little ammunition."

"And where would we go exactly?"

"North. Wick or Thurso maybe. They're smaller towns. They might not have been as badly affected and, even if they were, there's bound to be somewhere that we can find to settle. They're on the coast and in the sticks. We could hunt and forage and, if we found somewhere safe enough, farm too."

Jules picked up her glass and swilled the whisky around briefly then looked towards George. "Just like that, we pick up sticks and go on a wild goose chase for a place that might not even exist? We've got no guarantee that we'd find somewhere like that. Things up there could be just as fucked up … more fucked up than they are here."

George looked out of the window as the rain continued to pour. "The population of both places is about eight thousand. That's a fifth of what Inverness is. And I'm not saying we just pick up sticks and go. I'm saying we plan properly. We work to a timescale, figure out what we need and get it before we up sticks. If we can find enough fuel, we'd go on a couple of scouting missions. But I'm telling you in this place there is no future. It wasn't built to house people. I mean, dear God, have you smelt the drains every time it rains? And right now we're in the summer months. Can you imagine what it's going to be like in winter? How are we going to find warmth? That school today had everything. I probably let my excitement run away with me, but that doesn't mean there isn't somewhere else out there that would make a perfectly adequate home for all of us."

"So what sort of timescale are you thinking about for this?"

"A week to two weeks. It's important that we plan it right."

"And what sort of plan do you have in mind?"

"Well, it's going to be a hard sell after what happened today, but I say we get straight back on the bike."

"What do you mean?" Jules asked.

"I mean tomorrow we get out there. Maybe a couple of groups at a time. We need fuel, food, medical supplies ... as much of it as we can get in as short a time as possible. I know you seem to feel responsible for every refugee in Inverness. If we find any while we're out there, we'll bring them back, but then, when we're ready, we'll go. Leave this place behind for good."

Jules sat back in her chair. "What do you think?" she asked, looking at Maggie.

"I think it makes sense. If we stand a chance of surviving, I mean surviving long term, we can't do it here. I hadn't thought about Wick or Thurso, but I like that idea. We could still have polytunnels and grow crops, but we'd be able to fish, gather seaweed, forage for mussels and other shellfish. We wouldn't have to worry about starvation if the potatoes got blight or something like that. There are lots more possibilities somewhere like that than there are here."

"So that's two for."

"Are you saying you're not for it?" Maggie asked.

"I've only just heard about it, and to be honest my mind's still a mess," Jules said then took another drink.

"That's why what George said makes more sense than ever. If you don't go down there and show people that you're still in charge and that you have a plan, then we're going to have more disappearing on us like Stephen, Jeff and Clive." Jules let out a sigh and finished her drink. "Don't you think you should go easy on that stuff?" Maggie said.

"I'm going to go downstairs, gather everybody around and tell them that even though we lost a bunch of people today, they shouldn't worry because we've got half a plan. If you think I'm doing that stone-cold sober, you're as mad as this idea."

CHRISTOPHER ARTINIAN

12

The following morning, Jules remained in her makeshift bed for more than half an hour after first opening her eyes. She had not slept well. Nightmare images from the previous day had plagued her dreams, and she was dreading pulling back the curtain of her cubicle. She was convinced half the population would have left, despite her deciding to put a guard on the rest of the supplies. She stepped out into the aisle to see most people's curtains were still closed.

She saw Maggie and George up at the checkout desks and went to join them. They were with Ben and the remaining two conscripts in their ranks, Josh and Kyle. It was the first time Jules had seen Ben since she had heard about George taking a swing at him. His nose was bright red, and there was a small cut on his lip, but other than that he looked the same. He did not make eye contact with her but kept his head bowed towards the map that George had spread out.

"What's going on?" Jules asked.

"We're just dividing up the scavenger hunts for the day. In fact, we were just done," he said, looking at the three men, who subsequently drifted off.

"You've recruited Josh and Kyle? I'm surprised

they agreed."

"I didn't recruit them, they volunteered," George replied.

Jules rubbed her hands over her face and eyes to try to wake herself up. "So how many did we lose last night?"

"Most people aren't up yet, but I spoke to Andy and Rob this morning and they say they didn't see anybody trying to leave," Maggie said.

"Well, that doesn't mean much," Jules replied.

"You should go easier on your brothers. They're incredibly loyal to you, and they might not always get things right, but they try to do the right thing at least."

Jules let out a long sigh. "Yeah, I suppose you're right."

"I was surprised to see Ben here after yesterday."

"He was the first to volunteer," George replied.

"Guilt?" Jules asked.

"Most probably, but I can pretty much guarantee he won't ever make the mistakes that he made yesterday again."

"Yeah, you're probably right."

"So we've got four scavenger teams going out at once? You weren't kidding about getting organised, were you?"

George and Maggie cast each other an unreadable glance. "No, just the three teams will be going out," Maggie replied.

"So … who are we going with?"

"We're not going with anyone," she replied.

"You've lost me."

"People need stability. You being here gives them that."

"I'm not a fuckin' princess. It's not like things will fall apart if I'm not around for a few hours."

"You're not a princess? You could have fooled me, you've always spoken so eloquently," George said, trying to lighten the mood.

"Fuck you, old man," Jules replied, turning back towards Maggie. "I've never been someone not to roll my sleeves up and take risks the same as everyone else; it's not in my nature."

"I know that. Everybody knows that. The chances are you'll have to do that again at some point, but after yesterday and after announcing that we're stepping up the scavenger missions, George and I think having you here more will be better for everybody."

"So this is what the pair of you decided without even thinking to ask me?"

George folded up the map then sat down on the serving counter. "You asked me for help to organise all this, so I'm organising."

"Yeah but—"

"But nothing. This is what is best for everybody. Now, if you want to sort it all out yourself, feel free, but I spoke to each person who's due to go out there today, and they're all fine with what they're being asked to do. You being here is the best thing for everyone."

Jules studied him for a moment then looked towards Maggie, who had the same steadfast expression on her face. "Well, that fuckin' told me, didn't it?" she said, breaking out into a smile.

After breakfast, three groups of ten set out. There were five in each vehicle, two vehicles in each group. Their mission was simple, get as much as they could as fast as they could; help the group prepare for the journey north and the building of a new life. A heavy atmosphere continued to hang in the air of the Home and Garden Depot all day. People went about their daily tasks as normal, but the events of the previous day had unnerved them all.

Jules spent all her time on the shop floor with Maggie and George, making sure she was visible. Andy, Rob and Jon had appointed themselves members of the Home Guard. Each had one of the SA80s gleaned from the raid on the barracks and, despite Jules's misgivings, they were doing a good job, keeping watch and taking it in turns to check all the doors.

When the first of the scavenger groups returned, the mood lifted dramatically. All ten of them were in one piece. They had come back with vehicles laden with everything from food to camping equipment, including sleeping bags and airbeds for every man, woman and child at the Depot. Up until this point, only the odd few had sleeping bags and they were envied by the others. Most slept like street people on broken-down cardboard boxes, covering themselves with anything from dust sheets, the kind that decorators used, to canvas tarpaulins. Sleeping bags, though, they were a real luxury.

Jules, George and Maggie stood back and watched as the booty was brought in from the loading bay. The joy on people's faces was the last thing Jules expected to see after the previous day's events, but a knowing smile swept across her face and she looked towards George.

"What?" he said innocently.

"This was your call, wasn't it? You knew what this would do, what effect it would have."

George shrugged his shoulders. "I knew there was that big Blacks camping superstore on the trading estate just on the other side of town. Once I figured out a route that didn't involve heading through what we know to be dangerous areas, I thought it might be worth a visit," he said, bringing out his tobacco. He stopped and looked at Maggie.

"Go on, you old codger, I think you deserve it after this, don't you?" He smiled and proceeded to fill the chamber of his pipe and light it, taking a deep suck on the mouthpiece.

Josh walked up to the three of them, smiling. "It's good to see happy faces again."

"You didn't run into any trouble?" Jules asked.

"There were a few streets that we had to speed down, those things are everywhere, but as we got out of town, it got quieter. I'd like to head back out there tomorrow."

"Why?" Jules asked, unable to drag her eyes away from all the happy faces as they collected their new bedding.

"Jules, there is so much there that we could make use of. I mean we loaded what we could, things like dynamo lanterns, camping stoves, that kind of thing, but I'd like to go back with the other two groups and clear the place out. It's like a one-stop-shop for the apocalypse. They've got solar panels, all sorts of clothes and footwear. I mean, come winter, we're going to need thick jackets; we're going to need to stay warm. I'm telling you, that place could set us up."

Josh's enthusiasm was infectious. "What do you think?" she asked, turning towards George and Maggie.

"I think Josh makes an excellent point," George replied.

"Okay. Tomorrow, head back out there. Take the other two groups with you, but the same order stands. You get as much as a whiff of trouble and you get out of there pronto."

"Don't worry, Jules, I'm no hero. If I so much as sniff an infected, I'm out of there," he said, smiling.

"Good. How did the other thing go?"

Josh suddenly looked sombre. "We did the best we could. There was a small park near the trading estate. We didn't take any risks; we watched it for a while before we moved. Then we laid him underneath a thick growth of bushes. It was a nice park ... quiet. I—" he broke off, a little embarrassed.

"I said the Lord's Prayer for him. I don't really know much else, but I think he deserved a few words at least."

Jules reached across and took Josh's hand. "Scotty would have appreciated that darlin', thank you."

"Seemed like the least I could do."

"No, the least you could do is nothing. That was something."

There was a clatter, and all their heads turned at the same time.

Ben was the first to walk through the doors from the loading bay, and the rest of his team followed. He marched straight up to where Jules, George, Maggie and Josh were standing. "Well, if nothing else, we've got the biggest supply of chocolate bars and snacks in Scotland now," he said, looking at George, still struggling to make eye contact with Jules.

"And fuel?" George asked.

"We did as you said, but the tanks were dry. Rog mentioned something the other night about the army requisitioning all available fuel in the area before the withdrawal to London. I thought that might have meant from petrol plants, not bloody petrol stations. We got plenty of empty jerricans; we must have hit every fuel station in a ten-mile radius. We managed to siphon a bit of diesel from a truck but not much."

"Oh well, you did your best."

"Sorry it's not better news."

"I'd like you to go out with Josh tomorrow," Jules said, glaring towards Ben.

"No worries," he said, turning and walking back to the rest of his group as they handed out sweets and chocolate to the children who thought Christmas had come early.

Within half an hour, Kyle's group arrived back at the Home and Garden Depot too. Jules, George and Maggie walked out onto the loading dock to meet them.

Kyle climbed down from the cab of the box van and walked across to them. "Err ... there was a bit of a wrinkle in the plan," he said as he approached them.

"What kind of a wrinkle?" Jules asked.

The rear doors to the box van opened, and a procession of hungry, ragged-looking people began to climb down. "This kind."

"Jesus! They don't look like they've had a bite to eat

since this thing started," Jules said.

"Yeah, I think that's actually the case with some of them." He turned to look at George. "All the fuel stations we could get to in the outlying areas were bone dry, but there was some good news."

"And what would that be?" Jules asked.

"We found a water truck."

"What kind of a water truck?"

"The kind that delivers those big bottles to offices for the chilled dispensers."

"So that's what the transit's full of anyway."

"Well, that's something. Josh had a good haul too. I want you to go out with him tomorrow."

"Yeah, sure, whatever you need," Kyle said and disappeared inside the building.

Jules, George and Maggie watched as the hungry and sad-looking faces filed past them. More mouths to feed, more bodies to transport north, but if they didn't help them, who would? The three of them looked at each other, all sharing the same thoughts and all hating themselves at the same time.

The apocalypse had taken virtually everything they had. How long would it be before it took the last vestiges of their humanity as well?

13

Jules pulled the curtain across her cubicle and looked at her newly acquired airbed and sleeping bag in the glow of her dynamo lantern. It was amazing what the gift of three simple things had done for the morale of everyone in the place. Josh had brought a bulk stock of everything, knowing full well more people would be joining their ranks, so even the new arrivals were able to bed down in comfort, although Jules was fairly certain that most of them would have happily slept on beds of nails in exchange for a few morsels of food.

She peeled off her T-shirt, boots, jeans and socks before climbing into bed; she could see the glow of lantern lights up and down the row, and it made her smile. They had lived in the dark for so long that now they had them, people just kept them on for comfort, a symbol of some kind of civilisation at least. The front windows had all been doused with thick paint on the first day, barring one lookout window, which had a thick tarpaulin secured over it. This was peeled back during the day, but the majority of illumination came from the numerous skylights in the corrugated steel roof.

Jules flicked her own lantern off and snuggled into

her sleeping bag, which was now a few inches off the cold floor thanks to the airbed. Before tonight, she had just a piece of cardboard to lie on and a thin curtain to cover herself with, refusing to have any luxury that the rest of them did not share. A smile crept across her face. It had been some time since she had closed her eyes in such comfort. It did not take long for weariness to pull her into the first stages of sleep, and she was about to drift off when, suddenly, she felt a presence.

She opened her eyes and could see the silhouette of a figure crouched down over her bed. She quickly reached for the lantern and turned it on.

"Ben?" she whispered. "What are you doing here?"

His eyes seemed dazzled by the light, and when he opened his mouth to speak, she could smell booze on his breath and his slurring words suggested he had consumed plenty.

"I wanted to…" He started too loudly and, despite his drunkenness, had the good sense to lower his voice. "I wanted to apologise to you."

"At eleven-thirty at night, while you're pissed?"

"I should have come sooner."

"Do you think?"

"I'm sorry."

"Look, go to bed, you already apologised to me yesterday. We can talk about this tomorrow."

He looked at her, his head nodding back and forth like one of those toy dogs on a car dashboard. He was struggling to focus, and Jules had no idea with the state he was in how he had even managed to find her cubicle, but there was a glint of understanding in his eyes. "Okay, but I need you to know I am sorry."

"Alright. Goodnight," she said.

He slowly stumbled to his feet, pulled back the tarpaulin covering Jules's cubicle, and disappeared as quickly as he had arrived. Jules lay there awake, looking at the underside of the orange metal shelving above her. She had liked Ben, even though she knew nothing serious could ever come of it she had liked him, but now when she saw him, he was like a stranger. She did not hate him; she just felt indifference towards him.

The light of the lantern gradually began to fade and her eyes started to close once again.

*

When she woke the next morning, a thin smile adorned her face. Her back and neck were not stiff, and the rest of her body did not feel like it had spent the night in a meat locker. She unzipped the sleeping bag and climbed out of bed, immediately putting on her clothes before drawing the sheeting back and stepping out to face a new day.

To her surprise, there were a lot of people already up. George and Maggie were down at the front of the store, but Jules could hear clattering at the far end of the building as breakfast was being prepared. Everyone had their own duties at the Depot and there was one group who did nothing but inventory the food and prepare it for breakfast, lunch and dinner. At some stage, Jules knew that they would have to start rationing in earnest, but for the time being, while the scavenger trips were bringing in fresh supplies all the time and while so many newcomers had been surviving on little if any food, they decided to stick to two meals a day with lunch thrown in for the children.

Breakfast usually consisted of a choice of tinned fruit, crispbreads with jam, or breakfast cereal with long-life or powdered milk.

Jules walked down to the front of the store to join George and Maggie. "We thought we might have to send in a handsome prince to wake you up, Sleeping Beauty," Maggie said, smiling.

"Why? What time is it?"

George looked at his watch. "It's just gone eight-fifteen."

"Jesus! I can't remember the last time I slept past six. Why didn't one of you wake me up?"

"Thought you could do with the rest," Maggie replied.

"Well, yeah. That was the best night's sleep I've had in a long time." George and Maggie smiled at one another. "What? What's that look about?"

"Nothing, it's just we must have seen a dozen people already today who've said exactly the same thing. It's amazing what a few creature comforts can do," George said.

Jules looked around the giant showroom as more people began to rise and make their way over to the breakfast area. "I'm guessing our scavengers are chowing down?"

"No, our scavengers are already well on their way. They set off at about seven-thirty. Before they headed to Blacks, they were going to check out the council yard where they keep all the snowploughs and other vehicles," George said.

Jules's brow furrowed. "What have you got them going there for?"

"Well, chances are they'll have their own fuel store and, even if they don't, those vehicles have big tanks, you'd think there'd be plenty of diesel to siphon off."

"So you've organised everything for me? Then why the fuck did I get out of bed? I could have had a proper lie-in."

"Come on," Maggie said, "let's all go get a bite to eat."

As they walked along, they spotted Rob, with a rifle slung over his shoulder, checking to make sure one of the emergency exits was secure. "Oh God, he thinks he's Rambo or something."

"Hey, stop being such a bitch. All three of your brothers have stepped up. They're taking the security of this place seriously, which isn't a bad thing. They were the last ones to turn in, and Rob was the first one to get up this morning. They've worked out a rota, so every day somebody's up with the larks checking all the doors. One of them sleeps in the food store to make sure nobody does a runner with any of the supplies. They're doing a great job, so leave them alone," Maggie said.

"My brothers are doing all that?"

"Yes."

"Jesus. I never thought the day would come when they'd get off their useless arses and actually contribute."

"Yeah, well, they have, so leave them alone."

"I'm with Maggie on this one. They've really tried, all three of them, and I'll tell you something else, if it wasn't me that landed a punch on Ben yesterday, I'm pretty certain Andy would have."

"The point is they're trying. They're not always going to get everything right, but they're doing their best. Not for us, for you. They see how hard you work to do the right thing, to make things better for people, and they want to help you. A few kind words wouldn't go amiss every now and then."

"Jesus! Alright, alright, I get it. I've been officially told off."

"Good then!"

"It's like getting a bollocking from my ma."

"No need for language like that, young lady," Maggie quipped.

They arrived at the end aisle where all the food was laid out on a line of pasting tables. Jules, Maggie and George watched the newcomers as some of them just stood there in wonderment. One woman, who somehow looked familiar to Jules, began to cry as she stood back and held her daughter's hand just looking towards the tables in disbelief. Jules went across to them and crouched down. The girl was no more than five or six years old.

"Hello, wee darlin', and what's your name?" Jules asked.

"Florence," the girl replied, looking wide-eyed at Jules.

"Well, Florence," she said, taking the girl's other

hand, "I'm guessing you're a Coco Pops girl. Am I right?"

Florence nodded her head twice. "I thought so. Y'see, I'm a Coco Pops girl too and I can usually spot another a mile off. How about your ma? Does she like Coco Pops?"

"Cheerios."

A broad smile broke onto Jules's face. "So, your ma likes Cheerios. Come on then, let's go see what we can find." Jules led the little girl by the hand, who in turn led her mother. They walked along the row of tables until they reached the breakfast cereals. Jules grabbed three bowls, filled two with Coco Pops and a third with Cheerios, and then poured milk into all of them. She collected spoons, handed the girl and her mother their respective bowls, and then guided them over to one of the many sets of white garden chairs and tables that had been assembled for people to eat the communal breakfast in comfort.

Jules sat down with Florence and her mother at one of the vacant tables. "Th-thank you," stuttered the woman, eventually.

"You're welcome. Get used to this, we do this every morning."

"I'm sorry," said the woman, wiping her tears away. "What must you think of me?"

"You'd be amazed how many people have your reaction the first time they see this. But you're here with us now and you'll need to get used to it. Everybody here gets given a job, everybody contributes, and so everybody deserves to have food in their bellies."

"It's ... it's nothing short of a miracle. I thought we were going to starve out there."

Florence looked up from her bowl then just as quickly started shovelling the sweet cereal in her mouth once again. "Yeah, well, you don't have to think about that anymore. I know this little cutey-pie is Florence, but I didn't catch your name."

"I'm sorry. My name's Zeta."

"Huh, like that singer, Zeta Newman," Jules said smiling; then the smile suddenly vanished as the woman flushed red. "Oh my God, that's you, isn't it?"

The woman continued to look embarrassed. "It was ... once."

"How—how did you end up here?"

"It's a long story."

"Yeah, no doubt."

Zeta put a spoonful of food into her mouth and slowly chewed it, wondering where to begin. She looked down towards her daughter, knowing there were secrets she did not want to utter in front of her. "I ... err…"

"I tell you what. You and I will have a chin wag, later, how about that?"

Zeta's face lit up. "That would be nice."

Jules looked around. Everybody else was just enjoying their breakfast, oblivious to the fact they had a bona fide hit songstress in their midst. Granted it had been a few years since she'd been in the charts with anything and recent times had not been kind to her, but Jules was still a little dumbstruck that here, sitting on a white plastic chair with her knees almost touching Jules's, was a woman who she had mimed in the mirror to as a teenager. "I'll let you enjoy your breakfast with your daughter. You don't need to worry about anything now, you're with us."

"Thank you."

Jules stood and carried her bowl over to the table where George and Maggie had settled. "Making new friends?" Maggie said.

"You won't believe who that is."

"Who?" Maggie asked.

"Zeta Newman."

"Who?"

"She had that big hit with *Love on a Cloud*; then there was that other one, oh … what was it called?"

"I've got no idea what you're on about. Remember you and I grew up listening to very different things."

"Yeah, but I mean that was like huge."

"Nope, don't recall it at all."

"How about you?" Jules asked, looking at George.

"Don't ask me about stuff like that. I was never that into music."

"Bloody philistines. We've got a genuine pop star in our midst, and I may as well be talking to people who've spent the last twenty years in a grass hut with no electricity," Jules said, dipping the spoon into her bowl and piling a dangerously high pyramid of Coco Pops in her mouth.

"See this is the problem when you form friendships with people who aren't your own age. It's another good reason you should start spending more time with your brothers, I'm sure they'd be interested in hearing all about your new pop star friend," Maggie said, smiling.

With a mountain of cereal still in her mouth, Jules tried to respond, "Phwook you, y'old bag."

"Sorry, dear, I didn't quite catch that, what did you say?"

Jules raised her middle finger in response, and they all laughed.

The three of them sat at the table for several minutes, just watching everyone, particularly the newcomers. This morning, like no other, there were a lot more smiles, the mood was noticeably more optimistic. It was a combination of things. The airbeds and sleeping bags had obviously played a significant part, but the influx of newcomers had raised everybody's spirits too. It had made them realise just how lucky they had been and how lucky they were. Life was not perfect, in fact, life was a long way from perfect, but they had something special here. Everybody had a place, and to see the new arrivals in awe of their surroundings made them all incredibly thankful.

Suddenly, Mary Stolt, the woman in charge of the catering side of the operation, took a spatula and banged it hard on one of the serving tables three times, gaining everybody's attention. The entire makeshift cafe fell silent, and all eyes shot towards her. "Now, this isn't something we will be doing every day, so don't get used to it, but my team were up extra early this morning to make sure the scavenger groups went out with food and flasks. While you were all still in your comfortable new sleeping bags, we were boiling water, and I'm happy to announce that this morning, to finish your breakfasts, everyone may have a single cup of coffee."

There was a rush from the tables that made the opening morning of a Harrods half-price sale look like the overdue books line at a village library. Jules, Maggie and George watched with huge grins on their faces. Everything could have taken a huge downturn after the disastrous visit to the boarding school, but thanks to the work of George, Maggie, Josh and now Mary, people had all but forgotten the tragedy.

While the other servers dished out mugs of instant coffee with long-life milk, Mary walked around from the counter with a tray carrying three travel mugs, three plastic stirrers and several catering sachets of sugar. She placed the tray down on the table in front of Jules, George and Maggie then sat down herself.

"How to win friends and influence people," Jules said, still smiling.

"I thought it was the least we could do. Since Josh brought those camp stoves in yesterday and all the rest of that gear, it seemed a shame not to put them to good use."

"Well, you've certainly done that," Jules replied.

"I wasn't sure how you three took yours, but I was pretty certain you wouldn't have time to sit here lollygagging, so I put them in travel mugs for you. Don't get too excited, it's only instant, but it does the trick."

Jules screwed off the top of her mug and inhaled deeply. "Mary, you're a Godsend, has anyone ever told you that?"

"Plenty."

"Well, now I'm telling you." Jules closed her eyes

and took a sip. "I had the best sleep I've had in a long time, and now I wake up to Coco Pops and coffee. I could get used to this."

"Yes, well, I thought it would be good for morale."

"That it is. Look at those faces. People think Christmas has come."

"Well, I can't sit around here talking to the likes of you all day, there's always plenty of work to do," Mary said, standing up and heading back behind the counter.

"Nice talking to you too," Jules said, but either the sarcasm was lost on her, or she didn't hear the words above the sound of the excited chatter. Jules took another sip of her coffee as she watched the line of people gratefully take their mugs. She looked across towards George and Maggie; she could tell they were feeling the same satisfaction. *This has the makings of a great day*, she thought to herself.

She spent the rest of the morning mingling with the newcomers, talking to Zeta, and getting very few of her chores done. It didn't matter though. Jules had worked non-stop since they had first arrived at the Home and Garden Depot, and she deserved a morning like this.

She met up with Maggie and George again in the early afternoon, and they all sat at the same table where they had shared breakfast. The three of them watched happily as the children were served their lunches. Suddenly, the sound of a woman's scream carved through every conversation in the building, rendering the whole store silent but for the last echoes of the shriek.

Jules shot to her feet, knocking her chair over, and as another scream rang out, she knew that the happiness had just been an illusion that everybody, including herself, had wilfully believed.

14

Jules led the charge towards the direction of the noise. She did not look back but heard other chairs being pulled out from beneath tables and feet following hers. As she rounded the corner of the top aisle, she saw a small crowd gathered around the entrance to the warehouse. When she finally reached them, she understood the scream. The scavenger teams had arrived back. Ben and Josh were both covered in blood, but it wasn't their own. They were carrying an older man whose eyes were closed and skin was getting paler by the second. His body was riddled with gunshot wounds.

"What the fuck happened?" cried Jules as she looked beyond Ben and Josh towards the rest of the procession following them from the loading dock. There were several more wounded and bloody trails streaked across the floor.

"I'll tell you later, we've got wounded," Josh said.

Jules was horrified and confused and scared, but she could see the look in Josh's eyes. He was all of that and more. "Okay, get them down to the cash office. Get the ones who have the worst wounds inside." She turned around and caught sight of Andy and Jon. "You two, round up all the medical supplies we've got. Maggie, find us a couple of people who've done a first aid course or something. Anybody who you think might be able to help." Jules spotted one of the kitchen assistants near the back of the small crowd that had gathered. "Kelly, go tell Mary we need boiling water, lots of it." Andy, Jon, Maggie and Kelly immediately sprang into action.

"What do you want me to do?" George asked.

"Don't leave my side," she said under her breath before turning back to Josh. "Okay, come on, let's get down there."

The line started to move again, and Jules realised that she did not recognise all the faces. Reading her look, Ben said, "We found some people."

"So I see."

They reached the cash office, and three patients were carried in. They were in varying states of consciousness, but none of them looked good. More were sat down outside and made as comfortable as possible. Jules organised another small group to fetch the wounded water and help them in any way they could until Maggie or one of her recruits could take a look at them. There were twelve people needing attention altogether. The three with the worst wounds were out of sight, Jules had seen them briefly as they had been transported into the cash office; she did not hold high hopes. Kyle had been shot in the arm, but the bullet had gone straight through and, thanks to Josh applying a tourniquet within a minute of it happening, the bleeding had more or less stopped.

Other injuries were sprains, cuts and bruises. There were three older people who had been with the group they'd found. They looked shell-shocked and exhausted as they sat in the plastic chairs outside the office. When everybody who needed it had someone attending to them, Jules and George led Ben and Josh off to one side.

"So, what exactly happened?" George asked.

"We found three scavengers wandering as we were

on our way to Blacks. They were out trying to get supplies for the rest of the group. They took us back to this little TV repair shop that they'd been hiding out in. There were ten altogether including two kids and the three old folks," Josh said, pointing to the elderly people sitting outside the cash office. "Yesterday, there had been over forty of them. They'd tried heading to one of the supermarkets to get food but ran into a horde of infected. You can imagine what happened."

"Jesus," Jules said, looking around at the bewildered new faces.

"Yeah, well, we took them with us to Blacks. Got one of the box vans half full when we got hit."

"Hit?"

"Yeah. Whoever they were, they came in guns blazing. Killed four of us before we knew what was happening. We put up as good a fight as we could while we got everybody loaded, but four more of us took bullets and we lost another three of the group we picked up this morning. They started following us, but we ran into a horde of zombies and they obviously decided it wasn't worth the risk. We got back here on a wing and a prayer."

"Jesus," Jules said.

"We've used virtually all the ammo up. To be honest, I don't think it's a great idea for us to head out on any more scavenging missions. I think the next time we leave this place, it should be to evacuate. If we run into that army again no way are we going to be as lucky."

"Lucky? You call this lucky?" Jules said.

"Trust me. I didn't think any of us were going to make it back at one stage."

Jules rubbed her hands over her face. "And these new people … do they have weapons? Do we know anything about them?"

"Well, three of them died during the raid. There are the three seniors, the two kids, and two women. None of them look like they've eaten in days. There are a mother and daughter among them. They lost their family to the horde yesterday. The woman hasn't spoken since."

"Jesus, I can't say I blame her."

"That's everybody in now," Ben said. "I'll get the box van unloaded and then—"

"I've been thinking," interrupted Jules. "When you've unloaded, take all the vehicles round to next door's loading bay."

"What? Why?" Ben asked.

"If someone comes looking, we don't want to give them clues that there's anybody still here."

Ben, Josh and George all raised their eyebrows. "That's a good idea," Ben said.

"Yeah, I have them occasionally."

"Right, I'll get that sorted," he replied, heading off in the direction of the loading bay.

"I'll give you a hand," Josh said, following him.

When they were gone, Jules turned to George. "What do you think?"

"About what?" he asked as they stood there, arms folded, looking towards the hive of activity in front of them.

"Do you think we should head out sooner?"

"Let's take a little walk, shall we?" George said, guiding Jules away from the area and towards one of the quieter parts of the warehouse. "Getting out of here and heading north depended on us getting more fuel for the vehicles. Food's okay for the time being, and I thought our trips for the airbeds and the sleeping bags would make people a little happier with their lot while the rest of the preparations took place. If we're not going out to look for fuel, though, we're not going to get very far at all."

"When you say not very far at all, just how far is that?"

"A few of the vehicles are pretty much running on fumes as it is."

"So you're telling me that right this minute we're going nowhere, and if we don't head out to find fuel, then we're going to be stuck here. We'll gradually run out of supplies and slowly die surrounded by a city full of the undead."

"Well, I wasn't going to put it like that, but in a nutshell, yes."

"Fuckin' brilliant. Well, there's no option. If Josh and Ben won't head back out there, I'm going to have to go. We need that fuel."

"I'll speak to them. I'll try to impress on them how important it is to the plan working."

"Yeah, good luck with that. I can't really say I blame them. If I got attacked by a small army, I'm not sure I'd be inclined to head back out there either. But, ultimately, we're damned if we do and we're damned if we don't."

"Ultimately, yes," George replied grimly and removed his tobacco pipe, carefully placing it between his lips. He was about to light it up when the sound of footsteps made both him and Jules turn around.

Maggie had tears in her eyes as she approached. "We couldn't do anything for them," she said, burying her face in Jules's shoulder.

Jules hugged her friend and gently rubbed one hand up and down her back. "None of them?" Jules asked, locking eyes with George.

"All three. We couldn't find a pulse for Marcus or Bruce as soon as they came in. Paul only hung on for another couple of minutes. They'd just lost too much blood."

"If we had a team of doctors and the most up-to-date surgery in the country, nobody could have done anything for them."

"Such a waste. Such a waste of good men."

Jules continued to hold her. "It never gets easier, does it?"

"It never does," Maggie replied, still sobbing.

"Look, I need to head back and check on everyone. George, take Maggie to my office, I'll be up in a few minutes."

"A pleasure," George said and stretched his arm around Maggie's shoulders as he escorted her down the aisle towards the offices.

Jules watched them as they walked away and when they were out of sight let out a shivering breath, doing her best to hold back the floods of tears she could feel welling behind her eyes. "Jules! Where's Maggie?" Kyle shouted as he ran around the corner.

"Why, what is it?"

"One of the women that came in has just collapsed."

"Come on; let's go take a look," Jules replied. "Maggie needs a few minutes to herself." Jules looked down at Kyle's arm as they walked briskly back towards the makeshift infirmary. "How are you feeling?"

"You really want me to answer that?"

"No. I was being polite."

Kyle smiled. "In that case, I feel fantastic."

"Good." As they reached the small crowd that had gathered, the woman who had collapsed began to rouse. She looked almost white as if all the blood had somehow been drained from her. A small child, her daughter, stood beside her looking fretful.

"I'm alright. I'm just a little faint. It's been so long since we've eaten anything," the woman said.

"Somebody, please see Mary about getting these people some food as soon as possible," Jules said, crouching down by the side of the woman. "My name's Jules, and who might you be?" She looked towards the young girl.

"I'm Daniella," the woman said, "and this is my daughter, Gretel."

"Gretel?" Jules replied, smiling. "What a lovely name." She turned towards Daniella. "Are you injured at all?"

The little girl was about to say something, and her mother grabbed her wrist to silence her. "No, I just feel very weak. I'll be fine when I've eaten and rested. We haven't really slept in the last day or so either."

"Then I'm not surprised you're feeling faint. Look, we'll get you something to eat, then we'll get you and Gretel settled in a bedsit."

"A bedsit?"

Jules smiled. "Sorry, force of habit. That's what I call them cos they're not much smaller than the first bedsit I rented when I came across here. We cleared out lots of the stock bays and put some sheeting around them so people could have a little privacy."

"That sounds like luxury compared to what we've been used to," Daniella replied.

A procession of people carrying trays of food began to arrive, proudly led by Mary. "Look," Jules said, "get something to eat, and I'll get you a couple of airbeds, and sleeping bags set up; then you can have a proper rest. How does that sound?"

"That sounds perfect," Daniella answered with a smile on her face.

The food was distributed, and Jules stood up, immediately heading off to arrange the accommodation for the newcomers. By mid-afternoon, the new arrivals were settled. They all had full bellies and gratefully moved into their luxurious new apartments, equipped with all the latest post-apocalyptic mod-cons, including dynamo lanterns, water flasks and car air fresheners.

For the rest of the day, little work was done with regards to the preparations for the planned mass evacuation, and Jules was still conflicted as to whether to share the insight George had given her with the rest of the group. After the initial excitement and flurry of activity as the scavenger teams arrived back, the reality of the situation had begun to dawn on people. The ones who had laid down their lives had not had relatives or indeed anyone close at the Home and Garden Depot, but still, they were part of the community, and their loss was mourned. At dinner time, there was a small gathering while the new arrivals continued to sleep, and Jules said a few words in tribute to the people who had given their lives for the benefit of others.

Soon after dinner, people retired to their living spaces. Considering how upbeat the morning had been, the day had taken a depressing turn, but hopefully, a good night's sleep would help Jules, George and Maggie come up with an idea that would get things back on track.

The soft glow of LED lanterns behind the plastic and cloth partitions slowly diminished as darkness fell and people started to put their heads down for the night.

Jules was about to turn hers off when there was a light tapping on the outside of the tarpaulin that covered her cubicle; she pulled it back a little to reveal Ben standing there.

"Can I talk to you?" he whispered.

"Now? I'm just about to go to sleep."

"It won't take two minutes."

Jules looked across to see sheets covering the opposite cubicles begin to twitch. She tutted and climbed out of her sleeping bag. "Come on," she whispered, placing a hand on his back and guiding him down towards the front of the store where a single lantern hung above the cash office door.

"I haven't been able to think about anything else since it all happened ... y'know ... the other day at the school. Everything turned to shit in a split second and I made a wrong choice. Then, by not coming clean, I made another wrong choice straight away. When I said I was sorry, I meant it. You and I ... we had something."

"*Had* being the operative word." As soon as the sentence came out of her mouth, she regretted it. She was not happy with Ben, not by a long way, but coming out with something hurtful just for the sake of it wasn't like Jules.

"I—"

"I'm sorry. I shouldn't have said that."

"I just want to try to make things right with you. I

want to make it so at least we can talk again, normally I mean."

Jules looked at him in the glow of the lantern. "Let's take it one day at a time."

"Okay, that's a start."

"Now, it's been a long and incredibly shitty day, I need to get a bit of sl—" The sound of a child crying close by cut Jules off in mid-sentence. "What the fuck is that now?" she said as they both left the small arc of light they stood in to go in search of the sound.

Ben flicked his torch on, but before they had the chance to stray too far, Gretel appeared at the end of aisle five, where she and her mother had been housed. Ben shone the torch beam towards her tear-drenched face and Jules ran across to her. "Mummy!" was all the little girl could say before breaking down in tears again. In Gretel's hand, there was a folded piece of paper. Jules took it and was about to open it up when a bone-chilling howl tore through the quiet like an axe blade through cookie dough.

15

Jules immediately straightened up. The sound was unmistakable. There was an infected somewhere in the vast warehouse, and someone else was being attacked. "Arm yourselves!" Jules shouted at the top of her voice. "Arm yourselves. There's one inside the building." There was not a man, woman or child who did not understand what the *one* referred to, and, straight away, lanterns were turned on all over as panicked chatter and stifled screams began to reverberate through the dim interior of the showroom.

"Jules!" Ben shouted, grabbing a fifteen-hundred-millimetre pitchfork from a *Best Buy* end and tossing it towards her.

Jules snatched it out of the air and began to run in the direction the sound had come from. Ben took one of the pitchforks himself and sprinted after her, leaving the forlorn little girl standing there, beginning to howl herself as the tension and fear became more palpable by the second.

People quickly emerged from their plastic-covered cocoons brandishing lanterns, torches, and a wide array of weapons ranging from crowbars and hatchets to broom handles and clawhammers. Then something appeared carrying nothing at all, followed by a second figure. Even in the dim glow of the artificial lights, Jules could see instantly that these … things were no longer her comrades or even her species. Their skin was a ghoulish grey, and in this meagre illumination, their eyes were black as pitch.

The beasts paused for the briefest moment, almost as if acclimatising themselves to the dim interior, or maybe it was just indecision as to which body to begin feeding on first. But then Hell did in fact break loose.

The creature that had been Daniella leapt towards a twelve-year-old boy who she had arrived with earlier in the day. The child stood there, the screwdriver he held in his hand forgotten as he instantly lost control of his bladder on seeing this flying monster hurtling through the air towards him. The speed and ferocity of the attack were so great that he did not even have time to scream. He gargled blood as tears pooled in his eyes and the rest of his senses finally caught up with what was happening.

The second beast that had followed the Daniella thing out of the cubicle took two long strides before launching towards a terrified looking woman, still standing in the mouth of her own shanty dwelling. The decorator's dust sheet that had been her door separating herself from the outside world still rested against her shoulder as she stood half in, half out, frozen in time as the horrifying events unfolded. The beast tackled her hard, and both figures went cascading into the cubicle, the dust sheet falling back into place like a theatre curtain at the close of a performance.

As Jules continued to sprint up the aisle, she heard Ben behind her shout, "Kill them for Christ's sake!"

Everybody seemed to be glued to the floor, unable to tear their eyes away from the unfolding horror show that was playing out in front of them. No sooner had Jules reached the scene and readied her pitchfork like an angry villager chasing Frankenstein down the street than Daniella pounced once more. The twelve-year-old boy had fallen still, the light of the lanterns thankfully too dim to make his tears glisten, but his fate was clearly sealed. Jules raised her weapon, ready to plunge the tines through the boy's head before he turned into one of these abominations, when the opaque plastic sheeting from where Daniella and the other creature had first emerged flew open once more.

"Fuck!" Jules gasped, spinning towards this other monster that now stood there in a similar state of wavering indecision as the first two. It had not been uncommon for lonely, lost, frightened souls to find comfort in the arms of others on the cold, dark nights in the Home and Garden Depot – much like Jules had with Ben – but on this night, comfort was the last thing these two poor souls found. Jules lunged towards the scrawny-looking beast before it got the opportunity to do the same. With a roar, she raised her fork and speared the creature's head. Two prongs disappeared through its eye sockets before reappearing at the back of its skull. The beast remained there for a fragment of a moment before slipping off the fork like a chunk of rotten meat.

Jules twisted back around, turning her attention to the boy once again; thankfully, she was too late. In the brief time she had been dealing with the other beast, the boy had opened his eyes, only they weren't his eyes anymore. The figure had started to climb to its feet, and as she watched now, Ben thrust his pitchfork up through its head. The combination of adrenaline and her former lover's powerful physique almost flung the young creature into orbit. There was a sickening slurping sound as its head left the prongs of the fork. Its body flew two metres back, landing heavily on the Daniella thing that had already taken a chunk out of its third victim.

Another terrified scream rose into the air from what sounded like the next aisle. Ben and Jules shot each other the quickest of glances as the same chilling thought clutched them both at the same time. Ben flung back the plastic sheet that the second creature and the young woman had disappeared behind. Bloody swirls decorated the inside of the cubicle and the thick tarpaulin that hung behind, but the small compartment itself was empty. *This was running away from them fast.* "You stay here, I'll head through to the other aisle," he said, charging through the tarpaulin before the plastic sheet even had time to fall back into place.

Just seconds had passed since Ben and Jules had arrived on the scene, but already it had seemed like an age. Some people were still frozen in fear in the mouths of their cubicles, unable to believe what was happening. Jules raised her fork again, ready to finish off the Daniella creature, but then, like a switch had suddenly turned on inside them, the rest of the spectators jolted into action.

Daniella, leaving yet another victim lying lifeless on the ground, leapt through the air towards Mary, who had been amongst the audience, just gawping in incredulity at what had been happening. Even now, as the beast flew at her, she stood there, unable to move, unable to believe. Then, out of nowhere, a man in his fifties let out a yawp and shoulder barged the creature, knocking it off course and causing it to crash hard against the sturdy metal frame of one of the giant shelving units. Not giving the monster a second's respite to gather itself, he dived, raising his homemade truncheon with nails through it, and then smashed it down into the creature's head as he landed. The Daniella thing did not rouse. One blow and it was all over, but that did not stop the man pulling his weapon from its skull and pummelling the beast's head several more times.

Another cry of pain soared from the adjacent aisle, and as more people joined the fight to finish off the other creatures, Jules flung back the plastic sheeting that Ben had disappeared through seconds before and dived beneath the tarpaulin. As she rolled out of the other side, the gory violence from the first aisle looked positively sedate compared to the scene of carnage that she was now witnessing.

"We need help in aisle three," she yelled as footsteps from all around the cavernous showroom began to slap across the linoleum towards them. As in the other aisle, people had come out of their small domiciles, placing their lanterns on the ground to cast enough light for all the living to see what was going on. It was common knowledge that the beasts, the creatures, the infected, the zombies, the things … whatever people chose to call them, had amazing vision at night. It was one of the reasons they were so lethal and so terrifying, not that they needed any help.

There were numerous battles going on as people up and down the aisle were fending off or fighting freshly turned monsters. How these things could turn so quickly was something that often made Jules wonder if there was more at work than biology and chemistry. She had come face-to-face with more than her fair share. She had glared into those jet-black pupils and felt the malevolence behind them as they stared back at her. She was a lapsed Catholic but had never stopped believing altogether, and now Jules wondered whether, if she made it out of this, she should pick up a set of rosary beads the next time they went out to scavenge … assuming she lived past tonight.

The shouts, screams, grunts and running feet all combined to create an arrhythmic symphony of the damned. It became hard to focus on any one sound, so it was instinct more than anything else that made Jules turn. The beast was already within striking distance and her mouth fell open as she desperately tried to bring her weapon up to defend herself. It was too late. The thing lunged and Jules's eyes widened to the size of golf balls as she realised her life was over.

Suddenly all the noise stopped. The only sound she could hear was her own breathing. She could feel her chest heaving in and out; feel the hairs on the back of her arms and neck ripple with terror as this startling realisation overwhelmed her. *Our Father who art in heaven, Hallowed—*

The monster's grasping fingers were millimetres away from Jules when the hideous thing veered off course. For a second, she could not comprehend what was going on; then she saw Ben, flying through the air like Superman rescuing Lois Lane. He and the beast crashed into one of the cubicles, disappearing behind the thick cotton sheet doorway. Jules was about to fling back the curtain when she heard the petrified scream of a young girl. She looked up to see Gretel at the bottom of the aisle, watching on in terror as a creature tore towards her.

Jules's eyes flicked from side to side, surely there was someone who could get to the girl before the beast, but everyone was tied up with their own battles. Jules started to run, hoping more than anything that Ben would be able to manage the monster alone. Her eyes immediately caught sight of a creature lying motionless on the ground. Ben's pitchfork stuck out of its head. He must have literally just done that before diving to her rescue. *Surely he had a secondary weapon?* The beast that was closing in on Gretel was an older man in life, not as fast or nimble as Jules, but she realised quickly that she did not have the speed to chase him down before he reached the young girl.

Jules hurled her pitchfork along the floor as if she was bowling a ball towards some pins. The four-pronged missile skimmed across the surface and Jules stayed in her bowling pose for just a moment before continuing her sprint after the creature. The fork began to turn then roll, bouncing off the floor surface; then finally it reached its target. Jules held her breath as it passed below the beast but then the creature's right foot caught underneath the shaft, carrying forward and smashing it against the Achilles of its left foot. The monster crashed to the floor giving Jules the vital seconds she needed.

She came to a skidding stop as the creature gathered itself. Jules swooped down picking up the long-handled pitchfork and positioning herself in between the monster and the little girl. The creature pounced, launching itself into the air in one giant leap. Jules edged one of her feet back to give herself the best balance and poise she could before thrusting the fork upwards. The centre tines disappeared into the beast's gaping mouth before breaking through the back of its skull. In less than the blink of an eye, it was all over.

Jules looked beyond the lifeless monstrosity at the end of her pitchfork to the battles that were still going on up and down the aisle. She flung the creature from her weapon with contempt, the adrenaline, for the time being anyway, giving her more strength than she knew she had in her. More people had gathered at the top of the aisle and hurriedly made their way down, weapons raised to aid those in need. Jules looked behind her to see that Gretel had now been bundled away to safety. Before she could say a word, a group of men, including her brothers, rushed forwards and began to attack the attackers. Jules's brain kicked into gear once more and she started to run down the centre of the aisle back towards where she had left Ben a few seconds before. Her heart lifted when the sheet he had disappeared behind was flung back and he emerged into the soft glow of the lanterns. He turned towards her with his hand held up to his neck then fell to his knees.

Jules got closer and realised what had happened. Blood, black in the artificial light, was trickling between his fingers. His face looked pained and was getting paler by the second. She walked up to him as he knelt down in front of her. The surrounding fracas and raging fights were all but forgotten for the time being. Jules placed a gentle hand on the head of her former lover as he looked up towards her pleadingly. His breathing was laboured, and his eyes kept opening and closing as if he was fighting sleep.

"I'm sorry," he rasped.

"I'm sorry too, darlin'," she replied, and tears began to roll down her face.

Ben's left hand came up suddenly. It was clutching a screwdriver. The blade disappeared into his temple, and he collapsed forward, still clutching his neck. There was a loud crack as his skull smashed against the floor; Jules watched the black treacle pool around him. In the end, he had done the right thing. He had saved her life, and more than that, he had freed her from the obligation to kill him.

She carried on standing there as the fraught sounds around her died down to sad cries and disbelieving whispers. She could not pull her eyes away from Ben's body, and it was not until she felt a gentle arm around her that she finally looked up.

"Come on, love. It's all over now," George said quietly.

Jules stared at him for a few seconds, the tears still streaming down her face. "No. Don't you realise? This is Hell, and damnation is eternal."

16

George grabbed a clean handkerchief out of his pocket. How he managed to keep a supply of clean handkerchiefs during a zombie apocalypse, Jules would never understand, but he dabbed the tears from her face and then handed it to her. She unfolded it and blew her nose. "Don't worry; I'll make sure I wash this before I give it back to you."

"Tell you what, you keep that one. I've got plenty of them."

They both shared a sad smile and looked down towards Ben one final time before George led Jules away, leaving Josh and Kyle to organise the removal of the bodies and the clean-up.

They reached the end aisle and Maggie came running up towards them, holding the piece of paper that Gretel had been carrying. "You need to see this," she said, handing it to Jules.

"Can't it wait?"

"I don't think you want to wait to read it."

Jules opened the letter up, and George took a Mini-Maglite from his pocket and turned it on.

Dear Jules

By the time you get this letter, I will be gone. I'm sorry I wasn't honest with you, but I was attacked yesterday when we ran into that horde. One of them got me. It wasn't a big wound, but I know there is something wrong … something inside me that doesn't belong.

I hope you understand; I just wanted to spend a little more time with Gretel. I just wanted to tell her that I love her, over and over until she never forgets. I know she will be safe here. You are a good person; I know you will look after her.

Please don't worry. I disposed of all the crockery and cutlery I used, so there is no danger of me passing this on to anyone else. I have taken thirty-two paracetamol and ibuprofen as well as some sleeping tablets I found, more than a lethal dose, and I will be gone long before the virus can take me, so I will not present a risk to anyone.

I hope you can forgive me for hiding this from you, but I know you'll understand.

Thank you for everything,

Daniella.

"The fuckin' stupid bitch. She honestly thought she could outrun this thing? What the fuck was wrong with her? She'd been on the road all this time. How didn't she know the only way you can kill this thing once it's inside you is by killing the brain? She put her daughter at risk. She put every last fuckin' one of us at risk," Jules spat then turned towards Maggie. "When they've got rid of all the bodies; when it's all cleaned up, I want every last man, woman and child down at the front of the store. I want every last torch, lantern, fuckin' birthday candles, whatever down at the front of the store. I'm never having this shite happen again."

Neither of her friends had ever seen such anger on

Jules's face as she stormed off.

*

Twenty-seven minutes later, every man woman and child was assembled around the customer service desk at the front of the store. Jules still had the same look on her face as when she had walked away from Maggie and George.

"Thirteen," Josh whispered to her and then walked back to join the rest of the assembled crowd.

"Thirteen!" Jules said loudly, looking at all the sad and tear-stained faces. "That's how many people we lost tonight, thirteen. That's not even mentioning the people we lost out there today." She held a letter up in the light. "I won't ever again let one person's fuckin' blind stupidity put us all at risk. We lost thirteen tonight, but it could have been every last one of us. She started unbuttoning her shirt; when she was done, she took it off and threw it to the floor. She pulled off her T-shirt and undid her bra, dropping those in front of her too. Jules slipped her boots off then unbuttoned her jeans and pulled those and her knickers down as well. She kicked her clothes forward and stood there completely naked. Her thick, red hair flowed over her shoulders and down her back for all to see as she slowly twirled in the light. Nervous mutterings started around the gathered crowd, and Maggie stepped forward. "Jules, sweetheart—"

"Now," Jules interrupted, facing the audience once more, "I don't care if you've got body issues. I don't care if you've got saggy tits, love handles, a hairy back, or a fuckin' One Direction tattoo on your arse. And you know why I don't care? Because these fuckin' things don't care. These fuckin' foul-smelling, flesh-eating bags of shite don't care. All they care about is whether you're living and breathing. And if you are, they'll do their best to make sure that you stop doing both. So, no more! All the men, over there now. All the women stay here. Every last one of us is going to strip off and get checked over. If anybody has a scratch or a bite, we're going to find out in the next few minutes. If

125

anybody here isn't on board with this"—Jules pointed towards the back of the store—"you know where the fuckin' exit is."

She remained there for a moment with her hands on her hips, naked to the world in the glow of the many lights that had been assembled. The audience had been stunned into silence and rendered immobile for the time being. Then Josh clapped his hands. "Okay everybody, you heard Jules, let's get this done."

The men all filed off to the right, a number of them picking up lanterns and torches as they went. Virtual silence reigned for the next fifteen minutes as people disrobed and separated into groups. Everyone was feeling something way beyond embarrassment, but each of them knew that Jules was absolutely right, and how could they possibly object when she had done what she did?

Maggie and Jules insisted on being the first to be examined then acted as adjudicators while the other women went through the same process. George and Josh did the same thing with the men, and when it was all over, there were lots of faces that had flushed bright red, but there were certainly no bite or scratch victims left on the premises. Everybody assembled breathed grateful sighs as they got to put their clothes on once again. When it was all over, they formed a single crowd and gathered around Jules.

"Right. That's us all clear," Jules said. "From here on, we take in anybody new, they have a full examination. Now, it's late, and we should all get some sleep, it will be another long day tomo—" The entire Home and Garden Depot suddenly lit up in a blinding flash as lightning poured in through the skylights.

There were sharp intakes of breath all around the crowd and as the thunder made the corrugated roof vibrate like a thousand timpani drums all being hit at once, some of the younger children and a couple of the older women let out stifled screams.

"Okay," Maggie said, taking over, "everybody get

some sleep." The gathering began to dissipate. Then, just as the final echoes of thunder faded, a downpour began the likes of which nobody had seen or heard before. The sound was almost deafening, and Jules, Maggie and George all looked up towards the skylights to see if it was, in fact, rain and not a billion ball bearings that had been dropped from the sky. As the lightning shimmered again, they saw the deluge and knew that it was going to be a long, long night.

"I'll see you both in the morning," Jules said.

"Are you okay?" Maggie asked.

"You really want me to answer that?"

Maggie threw her arms around Jules. "Nobody could have done more."

"We both know that's a lie. I'll see you tomorrow," she said, reaching across and squeezing George's hand before walking up one of the aisles. She stopped outside a double bay that had two thick pieces of tarpaulin covering the entrance.

"Jules," Andy said, surprised, as she popped her head around the corner.

"Can I come in for a second?"

"Course you can."

Jules stepped inside. Andy and Jon were getting ready for bed; Rob was dressed with his rifle by his side, a knife in his belt and ready for action. "How many bullets have you got for that thing?" Jules asked, nodding towards the gun.

"Err ... none. But I think it makes people feel safer seeing it than not."

Jules smiled. "Thank you all for tonight. I saw you. I saw you racing to the rescue again."

All three of them looked embarrassed for a moment. "What now?" Andy finally asked, breaking the silence.

"Now, I'm going to go to bed, get some sleep and hope tomorrow isn't an action replay of the absolute fuckin' nightmare that today was." She shuffled over to each of

127

them as they knelt by the side of their airbeds. "Goodnight. I love all of you." She kissed them on the forehead then crawled back out of the bay and into the aisle.

The thunder rumbled again. It was moving away, but there was no signal that the rain was going to stop anytime soon. Jules walked slowly between the two giant units of racking. Several torches and lanterns were still on behind the curtained fronts to the cubicles. She could hear hushed chatter behind some, muffled crying behind others. Jules could not remember a worse day since this had all started.

How many people were talking about running into the night and fending for themselves? Ten? Twenty? All of them? She couldn't blame them.

Jules rounded the corner and continued along until she reached the aisle that was home to her own cubicle. The thunder drummed once more, but it was far less foreboding. Eventually, she reached her bedsit and stepped inside, flopping down heavily on the bed. She did not shut her eyes, she just lay there, thinking about the day's events and listening to the sounds outside. Everybody had been checked, every last person out there, but now this place did not feel as safe as it once had. Like a ransacked house, it felt violated, like there was something missing.

Tears filled her eyes as she thought about Ben. He had saved her life. Despite everything, despite that small part of her that hated him for what he had done at the school, despite the coldness she had displayed towards him, when it had counted, he had given his life to save hers.

Jules turned over onto her side, blocking out the dim glow beyond the tarpaulin. She finally closed her eyes tight and felt the uncomfortable warmth as the tears drizzled onto her camping pillow. "Thank you, Ben," she whispered into the dark in the hope that, somehow, he could still hear her words. The noise of the rain drowned out her sobs as they became louder and, eventually, as the tears ran dry, icy hands dragged her into a nightmare-filled sleep.

CHRISTOPHER ARTINIAN

17

When Jules awoke the next morning, she did not feel refreshed. She felt like she had relived the events of the previous day over and over. She heard the rustling and shuffling as people threw back their plastic, canvas and cloth partitions to face the morning ahead. Part of her wanted to escape the confines of her small cubicle, and part of her was dreading to see how many people had vanished into the night never to be seen again.

Jules approached the cafe area to see Maggie and George already settled at a table. "We got your breakfast," Maggie called over, and a number of heads turned before turning back to their own conversations.

Jules walked across to them and sat down at the table. "Dare I ask?"

"Dare you ask what?" George replied.

"How many we're down this morning."

"Down?"

"Jesus Christ, do I need to draw you a picture? How many people left overnight?"

"Ah, I see," he said, taking a bite out of a piece of crispbread with a thick layer of jam smeared over it.

"And?"

"How many times have you asked this question?" Maggie said.

"Well, it's different this time, isn't it?"

"Why, because you had a meltdown and whipped your jubblies out in front of everyone?" Maggie asked.

"Well, yeah, and the loss of people in the morning, the attack in the evening, not to mention—"

"Nobody left."

"Rain hasn't let up," George said, matter-of-factly.

"Am I still dreaming? You're talking about the bloody weather after what happened?" Jules replied.

George let out a long sigh. "Jules, Stephen, Jeff and Clive were only ever interested in watching out for themselves. It was always just a matter of time with them. These people here," he said, gesturing towards the ones queuing at the counter and then to the ones gratefully eating their breakfasts, "these are our people."

"Our people? What does that mean?"

"It means that they're like us. They realise that they're part of something bigger, part of a community. We stick with them, and they'll stick with us."

"Christ knows why," Jules muttered under her breath.

"I'm sure he does, but I do too. It's because of you."

"Yeah right. When's my fuckin' coronation?"

"You can mock me, but it's true. People look at you, Jules, and they see someone like themselves. They see a young woman who's doing her best. And yes, she's scared and unsure of herself and she doesn't always get things right—"

"Stop, you're making me blush with all these fuckin' compliments."

George ignored her and carried on. "But they also see someone who puts others before herself, who will always try to do the right thing, no matter what, who's not afraid of stripping naked in front of a crowd of people to show that she's no better or worse than anybody here, and she's prepared to practice what she preaches."

Jules went quiet for a moment, letting George's words sink in. "So … what now?"

"So, I think a couple of days of normality wouldn't go amiss," Maggie said.

"Yeah, I could do with a couple of days of normality. A nice lie-in, maybe catch a matinee with my mates at the cinema, then go out on the raz, finish the night off with a nice kebab and then wake up the following morning smelling of vomit and doing it all again. You think you can arrange that?"

It was Maggie's turn to sigh this time. "Real little smart-arse sometimes, aren't you?"

"Look, I'm sorry, Mags. I just don't know what you mean by normality."

"We mean no scavenging trips, no trips out at all. We eat our meals, do our chores and just have a couple of days with no drama. We lost a lot of people again yesterday. Right now, they're in the back of one of the box vans that, by the way, is still parked around the back with the other bodies from yesterday. Maybe we should say a few words, have a bit of a service. That's what's meant to happen when people die. That's normality. Gretel lost her mother yesterday, for God's sake. The poor little kid doesn't know what's going on. For her, for everybody, let's just not plan to do anything other than heal."

Jules nodded slowly. "You're right I suppose, as usual. But then we need to sit down and form a plan."

"Oh, you misunderstand me. The three of us aren't taking the day off; planning is all we're going to do."

"Thought it sounded too good to be true."

*

They held a service for the fallen and more than a few tears were shed by everyone. Jules did her best to remain composed, but the thought of Ben sacrificing his life for her made her break down as she spoke a few words for him. Everybody lit candles and said their goodbyes, but after the service was over, the candles were all extinguished, rather than being left to burn out. Mary, the kitchen staff and two women, one of whom had been a teacher and the other a teacher's assistant, kept the youngsters busy in the cafe area with various activities while the rest of the adults carried on with their daily chores.

Jules, George and Maggie all adjourned to the manager's office upstairs. They sat around the desk; they each drank a toast to the dead and then they got on with the business at hand.

"So, I hope one of you has something, cos I'm all out of ideas."

Maggie and George looked at each other. "I did some sums," George said.

"Oh yeah, what kind of sums?" Jules replied.

"First thing, I went with Josh over to next door's car park and checked the fuel levels in the vehicles."

"Let me guess. We've got enough to get to the moon and back with some to spare."

George did not smile. "One of the key things we were after during the scavenger missions was fuel, and everywhere we went, we drew a blank. In a few of those vehicles, we're down to virtually nothing. Now, we could send a team further out, maybe to some of the farms to look for some red diesel, but if they come back empty-handed, that leaves us with even less. It's a big risk. Plus—" He swallowed hard and desperately tried to control himself.

Jules and Maggie looked at one another. George was very old fashioned, not the kind to get emotional in front of women. Maggie reached her hand out and clasped it around one of his. "What is it?"

"It was my brainwave to send those groups out. If they hadn't been out there, they wouldn't have been attacked. In all good conscience, I can't suggest sending anyone out there again."

"Those people knew what they were doing. They volunteered. There are always risks involved. We had no idea that there was an armed gang out there, how could we?"

"It makes no difference, it was my suggestion, and I feel responsible."

"Yeah, well, welcome to the club, I'll get us some T-shirts made. But if you're saying we shouldn't go back out there, what the hell are we going to do?"

George looked across to Maggie. "We've been talking," she said.

"Oh yeah, and?"

"I agree; it's way too dangerous to keep heading out on the off chance that we might find fuel without knowing any real sources for definite."

"I don't understand. Just the other day we were all agreed on a plan to get out of here as soon as possible. Get supplies together and head up to Wick or Thurso," Jules said.

"Yes," George replied, "but that was dependant on getting fuel and it was before the events of yesterday."

"So, we just stay here and slowly starve to death?"

"No. We stay here and live," Maggie replied.

"It's a sad fact that we lost all those people yesterday, but it does mean that the food supplies will stretch further than they would have," George said.

"Oh, that's good. I knew there must have been an upside to seeing that fucking horror show last night. Thirteen good people died, but at least we get their rations now."

"I didn't mean it like that," he said, leaning forward and unfolding a piece of paper from his top pocket and flattening it out on the desk.

"What's that?"

"Plans."

"Plans for what?"

"To turn the outside portion of the Depot into a smallholding. We've got the materials to build three decent-sized polytunnels, and we've the space left over to plant plenty of outdoor crops too. The walls will protect it all from the winter winds, and as far as seeds go, we've got enough to keep us going for years."

"Seriously? After everything we've discussed, after talking about the need to get out of here, you're now saying that we should stay?"

George took the piece of paper back off the desk, folded it up and placed it in his pocket. He looked towards Maggie. "We think it would be for the best," Maggie replied.

Jules stared at them both. "You were the ones who convinced me we needed to get out of here and now you're saying we shouldn't. Screw it!" she said, standing up.

"What—what are you doing?" George asked.

"Everybody's looking to me for answers, and I don't have them. One day we're doing one thing then the next we're doing another, and I genuinely don't have a fucking clue. So I'm going to make this very simple. We're going to get everybody together and have a vote. We're going to put both options to them and see what they want to do," she said, storming out of the office.

Maggie and George looked at one another for a moment, wondering if she was serious, then chased after her.

*

Half an hour later, the three of them were sat around the same desk, looking at one another. "So much for a couple of days of normality," Maggie said.

"Yeah well. It is what it is," Jules replied. "You definitely know how to do this, old man?" She looked towards George.

"I've built these things before. It's straightforward when you've got the right tools and materials, and we've got the right tools and materials."

"And you think you can grow enough to stop us starving when the tinned food supply runs out?"

"You wouldn't believe the speed stuff grows in a

polytunnel."

"And you're sure we'll still be able to get enough drinking water if all of a sudden we can't use the garden depot for collecting it?"

"We'll set something up on the roof. There's even more space up there."

"I hope you know what you're doing," Jules replied. All their faces looked grim. The rain continued to pour outside and for a few moments, they just looked at it lashing against the windows. "So that foul stench from the drains, the one you said was a public health hazard waiting to happen. What about that?"

"Look, I can tell you're obviously upset, Jules, but—"

"Upset? Why, because everybody's just signed off on an idea that is going to be nothing more than a long, painful, uncomfortably ugly death for us all? You said it yourself. This place isn't fit for human habitation. It's in a city surrounded by the dead. You sold me fully on the idea of having to act because acting was the right thing to do, and I agreed with you. I still agree; getting out of this place is the right thing to do. A lot of people, good people, lost their lives to that end, but now it was all for nothing."

"So why have this conversation now?" Maggie asked, immediately jumping to George's defence. "Why did you go straight downstairs and put it to a vote?"

"Because without you two on board, I can't do anything. And I can't take the burden of this decision myself, I don't want to. If you say you've checked the fuel levels and we're running too low, I believe you. If you say it's becoming too risky to keep heading out there on the off chance we might find more, I believe you. If you say that we've got a good supply of food, enough to keep us going until the first crops come in, I believe you. But the problem is when you said this place wasn't fit to live in, I believed you then too, and you were right."

A look swept across George's face like he'd just

been punched in the gut. "But—"

"The reasons we wanted to get out of this place are just as valid now as when we made the decision to go—"

"But—"

"But what?" Jules asked angrily.

A tear appeared in George's eye. "People died because of me. People died when we went to the school. People died when they went to the camping store. I can't have that on me. I can't draw up plans knowing that people might not come back because of me."

Suddenly the bluster and anger were gone as Jules looked across the desk towards George. "And these plans… How many are going to end up dying because of those?" she asked quietly. The room fell silent again for a moment until Jules straightened up in her chair. "Look. You two are the ones I trust more than anyone. You're always there for me. If you tell me now that you believe in your heart of hearts this is our best option, then I'll get on board, and I'll commit to it. Is this our best option?"

George looked her straight in the eyes. "It's our only option, Jules."

18

They did as they said they would. They took two days for things to settle down, for people to take stock. Then, on the third day, they got on with the task at hand. Every man, woman and child in the place got to work clearing, digging, building and planting. The rain had stopped only a couple of times, and by the end of the fourth day, the work and the climate had taken its toll on a few of the older members of the community. One of them developed a severe cough that threatened to become something much worse. Another started shivering uncontrollably, and a third collapsed from fatigue. All three were taken to the cash office, which had become the unofficial infirmary for the place. Mary Stolt divided her duties between overseeing meal preparation and making sure the inhabitants of the infirmary were looked after.

When they downed tools on that fourth day, the frame of the first polytunnel had been erected, and people could see things coming together. The constant smell from the drains had become something that they just lived with and accepted now, and despite everything people's spirits lifted a little as they saw George and Maggie's plan starting to come together.

Jules, George and Maggie assembled back in the office as they did at the end of every day. George had drawn up a tick sheet and together they went through everything methodically, discussing the progress the different groups had made.

"I think maybe two more days and the first tunnel will be finished. Then Maggie can start fitting it out while my team starts on the second," George said proudly.

"Well, so far so good," Jules said. "When you got that final piece of the frame up today, you could feel the mood in the place change. It was like for the first time people could actually understand what was going on, what we were doing."

"We'll make this work, Jules," Maggie said.

"I hope to God you're right."

"I am. I know I am. Well, I'm going to leave the pair of you, I'm bushed. I'll see you in the morning."

It had started to get dark outside, but there was still enough light in the room with the blinds open for everybody to see each other. This was the north of Scotland, and it stayed lighter in summer, much longer than the rest of the country. When Maggie closed the door behind her, Jules stood up and walked to the window. She placed her hands behind her back and looked down at the loading bay below. "Looks like the rain's stopping again."

"It's been relentless for the past few days. It's a good job we didn't have any teams out, wouldn't surprise me if there was flooding in the city," George replied, pulling out his tobacco pipe and lighting up.

"I'm sorry for the other day, George," Jules said, still not turning around from the window.

"Don't be. You were stressed. We were all stressed and there are no absolutes in any of this. We are right and wrong at the same time."

"How do you mean?"

"I mean," he said, taking a deep puff of his pipe, "it's right that we're staying here. It was put to a vote and people have decided that the benefits of trying to look for a way to remain outweigh the risk. That's not to say that looking for a way out isn't the right thing to do regardless."

"You're filling me with confidence, old man."

George smiled. "Look, it was the smart thing to do, asking the people. It was their choice, now you're back to your old job."

"How do you mean?"

"How many times did a memo come from your head office telling you about this decision or that decision that was completely out of your hands, and you probably didn't agree with it but, as the deputy manager, you had to go downstairs, put the company face on and rally the troops?"

Jules turned to look at him and let out a small laugh. "Every fuckin' day."

"Exactly! This decision has been made, and whether you agree with it or not, your job now is to rally the troops."

"So what, I'm like a fuckin' mascot or something?"

"Pretty much. Except I've never come across a mascot who uses profanity to quite the extent that you do," he said, smiling and taking another suck on the mouthpiece of his pipe.

"Fuck you, old man. I'll give you fuckin' profanity," she said with a cheeky grin. "Seriously though, how soon do you think the polytunnel and the rest of the stuff will start producing?"

"You'd be amazed. Things grow from seed remarkably quickly in those things. My pal had one, and within a few weeks of setting it up, he was digging up marrows bigger than rugby balls."

"Marrows? Jesus Christ. Marrows?"

"You don't like marrows?"

"Well, they're not exactly at the top of my list of most missed foods."

"And what would be?"

"I don't know … bacon."

"Yes, sorry, Jules, I'm all out of bacon seeds."

"Think you're funny, don't you?"

"Look, It's all about maximum yield and speed of growth. If you fill people's bellies, they're going to be happy, and you can grow a lot of marrows very quickly. They're rich in vitamins A and C and—"

"Alright, alright, I don't want a fuckin' history of marrows. But please tell me that's not your grand plan. Please tell me you'll be growing something else."

George smiled again and brought out another folded piece of paper from his pocket. "I was merely giving you that as an example. There are a number of quick-growing crops that we'll be planting. Kale, chard, spinach—"

"Stop, please, my mouth's starting to water too much."

"Aubergine, various peppers, onion, cabbage, green beans."

"Okay, okay, enough. You know what you're doing; I won't question your superior knowledge anymore."

He folded the piece of paper away. "Trust me; we can make this work."

"I do trust you."

"Fancy a dram?" Jules asked, walking back to the desk and pulling out the whisky from the bottom drawer.

"Don't you think you drink a bit too much of that stuff?"

"Are you kidding me?" she said, pouring herself a glass. "I don't drink nearly as much of it as I'd like to. She held the bottle up. "And when this and the other one are gone, that's it. I'm going to have to go into involuntary rehab."

George smiled. "Who knows what the future holds, Jules? This time next year, we might have our own still."

"Yeah, and this time next year, I might be married to Bradley Cooper."

"I don't know who that is."

"How old are you exactly?"

"Old enough to remember when gobby youngsters were given a clip round the ear for being cheeky to their elders."

Jules smiled and drained her glass. "Well, I think I'm going to turn in too. I'm jiggered." George took one last long, satisfying suck on his pipe and walked over to the window. He opened it and emptied the glowing embers out, placing the pipe back in his pocket. "What are you going to do when you've smoked your last tobacco flakes?"

"Well," he said, "I've got a few tins left yet, but when that day comes, I suppose I'll just have to deal with it."

The pair of them left the office and, on reaching the landing, George flicked his torch on. When they reached the shop floor, it was dark and quiet. Everybody had worked hard all day, and many had decided to turn in early. A number of lanterns remained on, providing people with just enough light to move up and down the aisles. Rob was on guard duty once again, and he waved as he did his rounds.

"I'll see you tomorrow morning. I just want to pop into the cash office to see how the patients are getting on."

"Okay, I'll see you bright and early tomorrow," George replied and headed towards his cubicle.

When Jules arrived at the cash office, the door was slightly ajar. She levered it open to see Maggie sitting on a chair in between two of the airbeds. All the patients were asleep and, on seeing Jules, Maggie rose to her feet and placed her finger on her lips before guiding the younger woman back out onto the shop floor.

"They've only just gone off to sleep."

"How are they doing?" Jules asked.

"Well, they've been given paracetamol and hot cordial. We had some cough medicine too. We're managing to keep them warm, and they've all still got good appetites, so fingers crossed."

"They were insistent that they wanted to be part of it, that they pulled their weight. I should have said no to them."

"It wouldn't have made any difference. That generation were a different breed. You could have said what you liked, they'd still have done their own thing," Maggie said with a fond smile on her face.

"I suppose you're right."

"Look, don't worry. They're tough buggers, give them a couple of days and they'll be right as rain."

Jules reached for her friend's hand. "Thanks, Mags."

"What for?"

"For always being there for me."

"We look out for each other; that's what we're always going to do."

The two women parted and each headed to their separate living space. Jules stripped down to her T-shirt and knickers before climbing into her sleeping bag. She lay there for several minutes looking at the orange shelf above her before slowly drifting off to sleep.

*

When she opened her eyes again, confusion reigned for several seconds. Her head felt fuzzy and she couldn't quite understand what had roused her from such a deep sleep. It wasn't until she heard a volley of terrified screams from both men and women that she realised that, whatever it was, it was not good. *Surely it can't be more infected. Everybody was checked.* She pulled her jeans and boots on and ran out of her cubicle, brandishing a knife in one hand and a torch in the other.

She was greeted by others who had clearly been shaken from equally deep sleeps. They were in various states of undress and readiness as they appeared in the aisle. They were carrying either torches or lanterns, and as the sound of screams intensified, they all began to run in the direction of the disturbing noise. It was not until they reached the end aisle that the full horror of what was causing the screams hit them.

Rats!

19

For a few seconds, they were all frozen to their respective spots. It was as if the very ground was moving. The large brown rodents were everywhere. People came running out of their cubicles with them stuck to their legs, stomachs, and faces; they were running over their bodies and through their hair.

The screams rose in number and intensity. Jules could feel a crowd gathering behind her as they nervously watched the spectacle, as they saw the moving carpet coming nearer all the time. Then she saw something that she knew she would not forget until her dying day.

Maggie stumbled out from her living space, screeching at the top of her voice. Flaps of skin were already hanging off her face where sharp teeth had torn at her. There was a fat rat tangled in her hair, gnawing her scalp. She was adorned in just a T-shirt and knickers as Jules had been a moment before, and more was the pity as the rats became increasingly excited by the sight of bare flesh. They ran up her legs, sinking razor-like incisors into the fatty white flesh of her thighs.

Others bit her feet and ankles; then, suddenly, Maggie fell to her knees. Despite more than a dozen different battles going on with these hideous, foul-smelling creations, Jules could only focus on one. She was paralysed with fear. Her friend, one of the people she had come to rely on more than anyone, was being eaten alive right in front of her eyes, and the ever-increasing horde of rodents was heading straight down the aisle towards her.

Screams sounded behind her and to her side and suddenly the warm bodies that she had been shoulder to shoulder with seconds before were now gone, fleeing the scene in fear, but Jules could not move. She could not pull her eyes away from the unfolding horror.

The torment was not over for Maggie though. The rats continued to swarm over and around her. Two appeared simultaneously on her left and right shoulder, drawn to the fleshy, flapping lobes dangling so enticingly. In perfect synchronicity, the creatures ripped at the loose skin, tearing it clean off and making Maggie shriek even louder. She locked eyes with Jules. They were not the eyes of the friend she knew and loved. They were the eyes of a torture victim. A woman who just wanted to be put out of her misery, knowing full well that there was no road back to recovery from such a vicious and unrelenting assault.

Maggie's eyes widened even further as more creatures ran up the front of her T-shirt and finally her screaming stopped. Jules continued to look in her friend's eyes, but there was nobody home. The rats were mere feet away from Jules now, and as she saw her friend fall flat on her face, and disappear completely beneath the rampaging throng of filth, she knew that the same fate awaited her. She dropped her head and closed her eyes as tears welled and ran over her lashes.

Not long. A minute of horrific pain and degradation and then it would be all over.

The screams and excited squeals of vermin were suddenly joined by another sound. A strange, familiar whoosh. And accompanying the sound was a warmth that Jules did not understand. She opened her eyes once again, and the mass of diseased rodents was retreating. Some were on fire, and the smell of their burning flesh made Jules want to throw up. But the squeals of excitement had turned into squeals of fear. Jules did not understand what was happening; then she saw her three brothers and George slowly advancing. They had large canisters of insect repellent and lit candles in front of them—homemade flame throwers. The four of them moved forward methodically and slowly, forcing the rodents to beat a retreat. Some of the creatures began to scale the racking, only to be burned alive by a well-aimed jet of insecticide. Most scurried back the way they had come.

The men and women who were being attacked immediately realised there was some hope after all and intensified their efforts to fend off the creatures even more. Josh rolled up with a trolley full of various aerosols, and several men and women grabbed them, lit candles and also began to advance down the aisle looking for any stragglers. Jules did not. She remained in the same spot she had been glued to for the last minute, and as the furry attackers gradually disappeared, she looked towards the mutilated body of her friend. The bloody and tattered T-shirt hid very little of the agonising ordeal she had endured. Tears dripped from Jules's cheeks at first, then they began to pour as she realised she would never see her friend's smile again. She would never have her comforting arm around her shoulders; she would never hear her warm and soothing, motherly voice. Maggie, Mags, was gone now, gone forever, and with her, a little piece of Jules had died too.

Jules pulled one then another foot from their entrenched positions on the floor. She slowly walked down the aisle towards the blood-soaked corpse. The high-pitched squeals of the rodents and the pounding feet of their pursuers disappeared into the warehouse at the back of the store. The others who had been attacked, all in varying states of well-being, continued to cry out in pain, fear and disbelief, but for now, Jules was deaf to them all. The only thing she could hear as she walked towards her friend was her own heartbeat. Du-dum, du-dum-du-dum. "Mags … Mags!" Du-dum, du-dum, du-dum. "Don't leave me, Mags. You can't leave me." Du-dum, du-dum, du-dum, du-dum. Jules stood over her friend, hoping beyond hope that she would see movement, that there was some way back. Then, as if by magic, the older woman's shoulder began to move and Jules inhaled a shocked yet excited breath.

She bent down and was about to turn Maggie onto her side when the body of a rat that had got trapped beneath her squeezed itself out into the open. The creature, still a little dazed from the weight of the body that had fallen on it, paused for a second to catch its breath. That was its last mistake. Jules grabbed it and flung it hard at the breezeblock wall. The rodent squealed in fear as it flew through the air then fell silent as it splattered against the solid surface. Jules let out a scream angrier and louder than any that had already been heard before falling to her knees at the side of her friend. She took hold of Maggie's bloody hand and stayed there with her for some time. The clean-up had begun around her. She heard voices, she even heard her own name on occasions, but it was all in the background. The only thing she could see or focus on was Maggie.

It wasn't until later, much later, that she felt a warm, consoling arm around her and for a short time she allowed herself to believe it was her dead friend; but then she looked up and saw George there with tears in his eyes. He was kneeling too, and Jules could see he was feeling every ounce of pain that she was. "It's time we got her out of here, poppet," he said in a broken voice. Jules looked at him then looked beyond him to the assembled crowd. Her brothers were at the front, waiting to take Maggie's body away.

Jules looked down. Maggie's hand was still in hers, and she gave it a squeeze. "Goodnight, Mags," was all she could say before George helped her to her feet and led her away. Among the stock of tablets they had found on their scavenging trips was a box of zopiclone, a powerful tranquillizer used to combat cases of severe insomnia. George made Jules take one then laid her down to rest on her bed. He stayed with her, holding her hand until she fell asleep.

20

The next morning, when Jules awoke, her head was fuzzier than she ever remembered it being. She slapped her tongue around her mouth to see if she could taste alcohol or, worse still, vomit, but she could taste neither, it just felt furry. She desperately tried to remember back to the events of the previous evening; then they hit her like a juggernaut. Rats! She rolled out of bed and climbed to her feet, immediately feeling woozy and needing to grab hold of the cold, orange, metal racking supports. She closed her eyes and took a deep breath then peeled back the tarpaulin covering her cubicle and stepped out to face the morning.

She did not quite understand what was going on as she made her way down the aisle, but people were removing the sheets and covers from their cubicles and placing them on the shelves above. She could feel her body swaying from side to side as she walked and still struggled to believe that she had not had an excess of alcohol the night before. Stepladders were being erected, and something was being painted onto the support legs of the giant warehouse racks.

Was she still dreaming? All of this seemed so bizarre. She reached the end aisle and then George came rushing towards her. It took Jules a moment to focus, but then she saw dark, heavy rings beneath his eyes, and finally, everything came rushing back to her. She instinctively threw her arms around him and he uncharacteristically reciprocated. After a brief embrace, she pulled away.

"I remember the attack, but I don't remember much else."

"Well, it was your brothers who saved us," George said.

"Say what?"

"Your brothers. They came up with the idea of using aerosols as flame throwers to beat the rats back. If it wasn't for them, Jules, I dread to think what could have happened last night. We lost Maggie and two more, but if it wasn't for their quick thinking, we could have lost everyone."

"The rats, where did they come from?"

"Hard to say, but my guess is maybe the storm drains as they overflowed."

"How did they get in here though?"

"Rats are very capable and very intelligent. If they want to get in somewhere, they'll get in. We managed to chase them all out through the warehouse roller shutter. Your brothers remained on patrol all night, ready to raise the alarm if they came back, but they didn't, thank Christ."

"What's going on?" Jules said, gesturing back to the aisle she had come from.

"Well, as a precautionary measure, we're moving everybody off ground level. These racks are four shelves high, with an equal distance between each shelf. The upper shelves won't be as comfortable as the ones on the ground floor, but we're greasing the legs, so if those things come back, it's going to be virtually impossible for them to get up. We're moving everyone from the spread of the shop floor to just two aisles, so it's going to be a bit like living in a high-rise block of flats."

"Sounds great, people are going to love that."

"Listen, after what happened last night, people would live in a waste skip if it meant they didn't have to face that again."

"What's happened to the others who were attacked?"

"We've moved the infirmary to the meeting room upstairs. There's going to be a constant guard just in case. Some of them were really badly injured. We've given them some antibiotics, but, to be honest, without any kind of real medical knowledge, we're just clutching at straws."

The stress lines on Jules's face deepened the more George told her. "I mean, Jesus, rats. They're full of disease. God knows what we might be dealing with."

George looked down towards the floor as if something Jules said had saddened him. He reached into his pocket. "On the subject of Jesus and God, I know Maggie would have wanted you to have this." He handed her a gold crucifix on a chain. Jules held it up and watched it spinning for a few seconds before opening the clasp and putting it around her neck.

"I hope wherever she is now, she's not suffering."

"We should plant something, say a few words later."

"Yeah."

"She thought the world of you."

"She thought the world of you too."

"I'll miss her."

"Me too." Jules looked around as people climbed ladders and tied ropes to the upper shelves.

One of the children walked by with his mother. "It's going to be like sleeping in giant bunk beds," he said.

The innocent comment brought a temporary smile to George's and Jules's face, but it was just that, temporary. "So, this is going to be our life now? Scared to go outside cos of the zombies and armed gangs. Scared to stay inside cos of the rats."

"We'll get on top of it, just like we get on top of

everything," George replied.

"How? You got a past working for Rentokil that you haven't told me about?"

"Every problem has a solution, Jules," he said, gesturing towards the preparations.

"I suppose you're right. What are we doing to block entrances? I mean they must have come from somewhere."

"That's a tough one. There are gaps under external doors, there are the air and heating ducts, the drains, toilets, there are a thousand different ways for them to get in. They caught us completely unaware last night. I think we should concentrate all our efforts today on making sure that if they get in again, nobody gets hurt."

"That's probably smart. Okay, what about the food?"

"What do you mean?" George asked.

"Did they get to the food last night?"

A look of panic swept across George's face. "Oh God, with everything else that was going on I didn't even think about that." They both walked quickly down the aisle towards the back, and when they reached the food store, they let out audible breaths of relief.

"Right. We won't tempt fate, if those little fuckers show up again we won't be as lucky a second time. Let's get all this stuff onto pallets, I'll go get the forklift, and we'll load it onto some of the higher shelves. Mary might not be too happy that she won't have the same access to it, but it's better than the alternative."

"Have you got a counterbalance licence?" George asked.

"Do I look like the type of girl who'd have a fuckin' counterbalance licence? Look, wait until we've got all of this stuff out of here then you can report me to the Health and Safety Executive," she said with a smirk.

"I was only asking."

"Yeah, well, you should know better. Now go get some bodies to help us with this."

Everyone worked tirelessly all morning to make the building as rodent-proof as possible. A small group patrolled to make sure there was no sign of the creatures reappearing before the preparations were completed. After lunch, there was another small planting ceremony to pay tribute to the people they'd lost. George said a few words on behalf of Ben, and then Jules stepped forward to speak about Maggie.

"Maggie was like a second ma to me. She was always there when I needed her. She always picked me up when I fell down. In fact, I'm pretty certain that wasn't just me; that was all of us. She believed in this place. She believed we could make it work, she believed in the people here. When I woke up this morning, there was part of me that didn't want to face the day. We all know what happened last night. I was there, front and centre. I saw what happened to my friend. There was part of me this morning that asked what the point was. What was the point of continuing all of this? But then the answer came to me. Maggie. That's the point. She believed in us, and if I didn't carry on, then I would be disrespecting her memory. We all would. We're in hard times. There'll be plenty more ahead of us. I might get pissed off; I might get disheartened; I might need some of you to pick me up now and again," she said, looking towards George and then to her brothers. "But I promise you, while I've got a breath left in me I'm never going to give up. Now, there's still some work to do, and Mags would be the first one giving me grief if I slacked off." A small ripple of laughter circulated through the crowd. Jules smiled too then headed out of the small memorial enclosure.

*

People were tired but nervous as they settled down for the evening. They had a number of lookouts in place and more lights than usual, but that did not stop everybody being more watchful than ever. It was after eleven o'clock when panicked voices issued a chilling prelude to what was to come. The sheets, flaps of plastic and tarpaulins all peeled back as what seemed like double the amount of rats than had arrived the previous night stormed the building. The smell was horrific, just like that of the overflowing drains at the back of the store.

The brown bodies ran like a river between the aisles. Dozens of creatures desperately tried to scale the greased legs of the racking, only to fail in their endeavours.

If any got too high, a sudden burst of flame ignited the potential aggressor and acted as a stark warning to others. It was all working to plan, and, as horrific and sickening as the sight was, the realisation that while they remained high on the racks they were safe eased the tension in the air. But then, as a terrified scream instantly drowned out the high-pitched squeals of the creatures, everyone realised that something had gone wrong.

21

The sound had come from the far end of the racking system that Jules's shelf was on. She frantically began to move towards it, gripping the cold metal frame of the rack, invading living space after living space while people froze and huddled with terror. She swung and dived and crawled like deranged orangutan until she finally reached the end cubicle. Two rats were clinging to a young woman. Her child was huddled in a corner, petrified, while the beasts clawed and gnawed at her mother's arm.

Jules grabbed the first of the creatures, squeezing it like a shit-smelling sponge. The rat squealed with pain, releasing its grip, and Jules flung it over the edge to the ground before doing the same to the next. "How did they get up here?" she demanded.

The woman pointed to the racking against the wall. Nobody was living on that, and so they had not bothered to grease the legs. A number of the rodents had climbed onto the shelves and were attempting to leap across. So far only two had made it. Jules reached for the aerosol, candle and lighter that every living space had been issued with just in case. At that second, another two creatures launched themselves from the other shelving unit. Jules did not watch, she lit the candle, brought the aerosol up and fired. The two creatures were mere inches away when they turned into shrieking balls of flames and fell to the ground. "Okay, now!" shouted Jules at the top of her voice.

The woman and the child looked on in confusion, not understanding who Jules was shouting at, but then, multiple loud whooshes sounded and bright flashes of light lit the interior of the showroom as Molotov cocktails were flung.

The pained squeals of the creatures became almost deafening, and the smell of flesh cooking and burning was so strong that it coated everyone and everything like thick gloss paint. As the small beasts began to beat a retreat once more, the grease on some of the racking legs caught fire.

When the majority of the rats had disappeared, several small groups began a mopping-up process. They climbed down from the relative safety of their shelves and used the makeshift flamethrowers to kill and chase any leftover attackers.

A group of firefighters began to run around the showroom dousing anything that had caught fire.

The rats did not come back that night, but there was a feeling shared by everyone that they would see them again.

*

On the third evening, they arrived earlier and came in still greater numbers. All the legs in the place had been greased this time. The patients in the meeting room upstairs had been barricaded in, and a group of four guards all armed with flame throwers were ready and waiting.

Despite the efforts of the rats, they did not get near anyone or any of the food. When the Molotov cocktails were tossed, the creatures retreated once again. Despite the fact they had got through the night unscathed, a chilling darkness began to fall over the Home and Garden Depot. Was this what life was going to be like now?

*

The following day, Jules called a meeting in her office with the people who had all been key in drawing up and executing the plans to deal with the rat problem.

"As far as brainstorming sessions go," she said, looking down at the almost blank piece of paper in front of her, "this doesn't say very fuckin' much for any of us."

"In all honesty, I don't know what else we can do," said an older woman who had been one of Maggie's friends and now taken up the crusade with Jules to honour her memory. "I mean we're killing more of them each night, but still more appear. For the time being, I think if none of us are getting hurt, then that's a victory."

"If that's what we're calling a victory these days, that's pretty fuckin' sad. Look, we need to—"

"Shit!" Andy cried, looking out of the window.

All eyes in the room shot towards him.

"What is it?" Jules asked.

"We've got company," he said, unshouldering his rifle and charging out of the room; others followed, leaving Jules and just a small handful of her inner circle to run to the window and see what was going on.

They all watched from behind the blinds as a lorry came to a stop and two women climbed out, one with blonde hair, one with dark hair. They walked to the rear of the vehicle and unlocked the door. Two more jumped down, and the first two climbed onto the loading dock, disappearing from view beneath the canopy.

A steady procession of females of all ages gradually filtered out of the back of the lorry.

"Jesus Christ," Jules said as she watched the terrified looking crowd gather and turn towards the building.

"Where do you suppose they're from?" George asked.

"God only knows, but it doesn't look like they've had an easy ride," Jules replied, continuing to watch. "We'll know soon enough when Andy and the boys bring them up here."

The group continued their vigil at the window for a few more minutes, but then they all jumped as a panicked shout rose from outside the office.

"Jules, Jules," came the cry.

Jules charged to the door, followed by the others. Everyone who had a weapon on them raised it as they ran out into the large, well-lit reception area.

"Drop your weapons or he buys it, followed by one of you," the blonde-haired American woman who had been driving the lorry commanded.

"Jesus fucking Christ!" blurted Jules as she saw Andy had been beaten to a bloody mess, while Rob had been stabbed and now had a knife at his throat. "Lower your weapons." The others immediately obeyed. "Do you mind taking the knife from my brother's throat please?" she asked politely.

"Your brother?" the American asked, surprised. She looked towards the woman she had arrived with then back towards Jules. "Who are you people and what do you want with us?"

We don't want anything with you other than to find out why you broke into our place and get you the f— get you out of here," Jules replied. "Now, please take the knife from my brother's throat."

The American's expression softened as she looked beyond Jules towards the assembled faces behind her. She reached down and unbuckled Rob's belt.

"What are you doing?" he screamed, terrified this American psycho was going to torture him further.

"Do you have any bandages or medical supplies? I need to see to his wound before he loses too much blood," the American said.

"You're a doctor?" Jules asked, amazed.

The American nodded while helping the young man onto the floor. She took off the belt and carefully removed his trousers as he let out a whimper. She wrapped the belt around his leg above the wound to stem the flow of blood. "The cut's not too deep, I didn't hit anything major, but I'm going to need to suture it."

"Get her what she needs," Jules said to the others in the group as the room sprang into a hive of activity. She looked towards the unconscious figure with the pummelled face. "And can someone see to Andy?" she asked, looking to one of the older women. "In the meantime, please come with me," she said directly to the dark-haired woman who had arrived with the American. "Nice work you did on my brother."

"That was Lucy, not me, and anyway, he had it coming. He was lucky to get away with just a cut," the dark-haired woman said, not feeling the need to justify their actions.

"Not him, the other one." She gestured back to the battered, unconscious figure who was being dragged across the floor for Lucy to look at after she had attended to her own victim.

"How many brothers have you got?"

"Three, the third is the one who screamed like a girl when you took out the other two," Jules replied.

"You must be so proud," the dark-haired woman said with a smirk.

"You have any brothers?"

"Two."

"I'm guessing you love them more than anything, but that doesn't stop them from being a constant pain in the fuckin' tits."

"One of them's only six and he's adorable, but it sounds like you've already met the other... My name's Emma," she said, extending a hand as they entered the office from where the group had emerged.

"Aren't we fucking formal now?" Smiling, Jules extended her hand and curtseyed. "Delighted to meet you, Emma, my name's Julia, but everyone calls me Jules," she said in an affected English accent before falling back into her friendly Belfast one. "So, do you mind telling me who the fuck you are? And what the fuck are you doing here?"

The Beginning

A NOTE FROM THE AUTHOR

I really hope you enjoyed this book and would be very grateful if you took a minute to leave a review on Amazon and Goodreads.

If you would like to stay informed about what I'm doing, including current writing projects, and all the latest news and release information; these are the places to go:

Join the fan club on Facebook
https://www.facebook.com/groups/127693634504226

Like the Christopher Artinian author page
https://www.facebook.com/safehaventrilogy/

Buy exclusive and signed books and merchandise, subscribe to the newsletter and follow the blog:
https://www.christopherartinian.com/

Follow me on Twitter
https://twitter.com/Christo71635959

Follow me on Amazon
https://amzn.to/2I1llU6

Follow me on Goodreads
https://bit.ly/2P7iDzX

Other books by Christopher Artinian:

Safe Haven: Rise of the RAMs
Safe Haven: Realm of the Raiders
Safe Haven: Reap of the Righteous
Safe Haven: Ice
Before Safe Haven: Lucy
Before Safe Haven: Alex
Before Safe Haven: Mike
The End of Everything: Book 1
The End of Everything: Book 2
The End of Everything: Book 3
The End of Everything: Book 4
The End of Everything: Book 5
The End of Everything: Book 6

Anthologies featuring short stories by Christopher
Artinian

Undead Worlds: A Reanimated Writers Anthology

Featuring: Before Safe Haven: Losing the Battle by Christopher Artinian

Tales from Zombie Road: The Long-Haul Anthology

Featuring: Condemned by Christopher Artinian

Treasured Chests: A Zombie Anthology for Breast Cancer Care

Featuring: Last Light by Christopher Artinian

Trick or Treat Thrillers (Best Paranormal 2018)

Featuring: The Akkadian Vessel.

CHRISTOPHER ARTINIAN

Christopher Artinian was born and raised in Leeds, West Yorkshire. Wanting to escape life in a big city and concentrate more on working to live than living to work, he and his family moved to the Outer Hebrides in the north-west of Scotland in 2004, where he now works as a full-time author.

Chris is a huge music fan, a cinephile, an avid reader and a supporter of Yorkshire county cricket club. When he's not sat in front of his laptop living out his next post-apocalyptic/dystopian/horror adventure, he will be passionately immersed in one of his other interests.

Printed in Great Britain
by Amazon